Cindi-
K

CRAVING THE COWBOY

Grape Seed Falls Romance Book 2

LIZ ISAACSON

Liz

AEJ Creative Works

ISBN-13: 978-1980423768

"Beloved, let us love one another: for love is of God; and every one that loveth is born of God, and knoweth God."

— 1 JOHN 4:7

CHAPTER ONE

Dwayne Carver sat in the cab of his truck, taking an extra moment to prepare to get out for two reasons. One, it was mighty hot in Texas Hill Country this afternoon. Two, he'd have to smile and laugh and converse with people for the next few hours. For a man who spent most of his time with horses, dogs, and his parents, what he was about to do definitely required a second or two to gather his internal strength.

He exhaled and reached for the door handle. The heat hit him square in the chest, making his breath stick in his lungs. He'd been coming to the Peach Jamboree and the rodeo in Crawford for as long as he could remember. Born and raised in Grape Seed Falls, just a short fifteen minute drive from the county seat, Dwayne wouldn't be Texan without attending at least one rodeo every summer.

As it was only June, Dwayne was getting his quota filled early. If only Mother Nature had gotten the memo that it was still early in the summer. He couldn't even imagine what August would be like this year.

He pushed the weather from his mind as his boots drank up the dust during the long walk toward the festivities already in full swing. He usually stuffed himself full of biscuits and peach preserves, fried chicken and waffles, and more sweet tea than a person should be allowed to drink.

But not today.

Oh, no. Today, he was sitting in the dunk tank, determined to hold down his record of staying dry for the third summer in a row. A bit of pride swelled his chest, and he worked to squash it. His dad always said pride didn't wear well on a man, and Dwayne couldn't rid himself of the life lessons his parents had instilled in him.

"There you are." Amelia Hardy approached, a round woman just a few years older than Dwayne.

"I'm not late, am I?" He didn't wear a watch, but glanced up at the sky like the sun would confirm that he'd arrived on time.

"Our last participant went under so many times, he left early." Amelia smoothed back her hair, the curly wisps of it making her seem a bit crazed.

"Well, I'm ready." Dwayne glanced over her head to find the area in front of the dunk tank empty. No wonder Amelia was frazzled. Each throw cost a dollar and the church used the money they earned from the Jamboree to fund their music programs.

"You're going in like that?" She scanned him from the tips of his cowboy boots to the silver cowboy hat on his head.

He grinned at her and pressed his right arm to his side as the tremors started to shake his fingers. "I'm not goin' in." He stepped past her, hoping his neurological disorder would quiet down. He prayed for it.

Just four a few hours, he thought. *No tremors for a few hours, okay, Lord?*

Dwayne climbed the ladder on the side of the dunk tank and balanced his boots on the narrow rail before sitting on the platform above the water. For a moment, he thought maybe he should pray someone would hit the button dead-on so he could cool off.

He swiped off his hat and wiped the sweat from his forehead. "Ready," he called to Amelia.

She picked up a megaphone and started calling for people to come "dunk the man who hasn't gotten wet in three years!"

Only a few minutes passed before people started gathering around, their curious eyes all lasered on him. Dwayne worked to keep himself still. It wouldn't do to show the crowd that he was nervous.

A boy no older than twelve paid for five baseballs, and Dwayne relaxed. He didn't have anything to worry about with a kid. The boy threw the first ball and it didn't even reach the dunk tank.

"C'mon!" Dwayne called good-naturedly. "You can get it here!"

Out of the five balls, only two made it anywhere near the tank, and that was only to bounce off the front of it.

A pack of cowboys came into view, and Dwayne's chest seized. His cowboys hadn't come. They hadn't. Kurt had promised he'd—

The man leading them turned, and his trademark white cowboy hat testified that Kurt had fibbed. Because not only had he come, he'd brought all sixteen cowboys from the ranch with him. And they were all holding cash.

Dwayne called, "Nice try, boys. I've seen y'all throw ropes, and I've got nothing to worry about."

"We're fixin' to see you dripping wet," Kurt called back, rotating his right shoulder as if stretching it out.

Dwayne scoffed, but a thread of nervousness pulled through him. He had seen Kurt throw a rope, and the man never missed. He wasn't foreman at Grape Seed Ranch for no reason. His skills with a rope were the least of his qualifications, and Dwayne watched as he huddled up with the other men.

An order was clearly established, because Kurt stepped to the back of the line while the smallest cowboy—Austin—handed his money to Amelia. Dwayne couldn't see the denomination from this distance, but Amelia held up the bill and proclaimed, "Ten baseballs for the handsome cowboy!"

She was married, but she looked and sounded absolutely gleeful at the amount.

Dwayne's chest tightened. He couldn't be dunked by one of his men. He'd never live it down, and every ranch function would become a constant ribbing of how he'd looked in soaking wet jeans and ruined cowboy boots.

He wasn't going in. Not today. Not at the hand of a cowboy.

An hour passed while his cowboys tried to unseat him, as the crowd surrounding them grew and swelled. Laughter and catcalls and cheers filled the air, and still Dwayne stayed dry. The platform wobbled with the last of Kurt's balls, which barely missed its mark.

"Awww," the crowd moaned in tandem.

Dwayne grinned at his men. "Maybe next year, boys." He inched toward the ladder, his back starting to ache, and his blasted right arm trembling no matter how hard he leaned into his palm on the wooden platform.

He'd signed up for a few hours, but he always got a break every so often.

"One more?" Amelia called, barely glancing over her shoulder.

Dwayne said, "Sure," as he searched for the next person who thought they could dunk him when a herd of cowboys couldn't.

The crowd stepped back and a woman met his eye. A tall, tan, raven-haired woman, who wore a black cowgirl hat with a red beaded hatband. With her long, jean-clad legs, the dark red cowgirl boots, and the canary-colored tank top, Dwayne had never seen such a heavenly vision.

His heart started pumping harder, and not because he was worried she could unseat him.

Who was she?

Dwayne had never seen her before, and he reasoned that he'd been out of the marriage market for a while. It was entirely possible that more females than he knew had moved to Grape Seed Falls in the past four years since he'd stopped dating.

He gripped the platform with all his fingers, watching her as her lips lifted into a smile. "You don't think I can sink you, do you?"

Dwayne lifted his left shoulder a couple of inches. Might as well be honest. "Not really."

She tossed the baseball from one hand to the other. Left to right. Right to left.

His elbow shook the tiniest bit, and he locked it. He didn't want this woman to ever know about his time in the military, which had led to his traumatic brain injury, which had left him with this trembling in his right hand and arm.

At the same time, he wanted a lot more time to spend with her, and if he did that, he'd probably have to tell her about himself—including his time in the military, the explosion that had changed his life, and why his right hand shook at random times.

Like it was now.

"How many balls did you buy?" he asked.

"Just this one." She gripped it in her right hand.

Just this one.

She was a confident little thing, and Dwayne's admiration for her grew. Still, she couldn't weigh more than one-twenty, soaking wet. And even that was generous.

"All right," he drawled. "Let's see what you've got." He wanted her to throw already. Then he could get down for a few minutes. Get some of that sweet tea he loved so much. Get cooled off. Take some painkiller.

She planted her feet and cocked her arm. She threw, and Dwayne only had one second before he realized her aim was dead-on. One more second before the ball hit the button.

And then nothing before the platform disappeared beneath him. Cool water enveloped him, covering him from head to toe. His leather boots hit the bottom of the tank, and he came up sputtering, water dripping from the brim of his hat and soaking his jeans, polo, and boots.

Laughter and cheering met his ears, but Dwayne could only stare as disbelief and humiliation spread through him like poison. He met the woman's eyes, and she ducked her dark cowgirl hat and disappeared into the mass of people.

On Monday morning, Felicity Lightburne woke with a buzz in her stomach that wasn't exactly comfortable. She glanced around the still-unfamiliar bedroom, disliking the butter-yellow curtains as much now as she had when she'd moved in last week.

She sighed as she dragged her legs from under the bedspread and sat on the edge of the mattress. Felicity wasn't bothered by the early hour. She was used to rising before the sun and being in the training ring with a horse by dawn.

She was used to sipping coffee in the dark, and smelling like dust and horse flesh, and showering in the afternoon just to get the layer of sweat and dirt off her skin.

But she didn't want to go work at a ranch without her father. Didn't want to work at a ranch that wasn't her father's.

"Couldn't stay there," she muttered to herself as she reached for the pair of jeans she'd worn yesterday. She could wear them again; all she'd done was wander around town and then attend the rodeo in Crawford. At least Grape Seed Falls and the other small Texas towns surrounding it possessed charm.

"Give me strength for this day," she whispered as she moved into the kitchen. She set the coffee to brew, scraped her hair back into a ponytail, and ate a banana before leaving for the new ranch where she was starting her new job. Apparently, the owner needed to hire out the training of the horses as the ranch continued to grow and expand. He'd hired her over the phone, and he'd seemed nice enough. Impressed with her credentials. Relieved to have her.

But none of that relief entered her system as she set her car west and left the town proper of Grape Seed Falls behind. She kept her arm draped lazily across the steering wheel, as if this was just another day at work. Just another commute.

But it wasn't.

Number one, she'd never commuted to work. She got up and walked out of the rambler where she'd grown up, crossed a few hundred yards, and entered the stables.

Number two, she'd never worked for anyone else. Her family's cattle ranch sat just outside of Dallas, and she'd worked the land there and learned to train horses from the greatest trainer Texas had ever seen. Her dad.

His death punched her right in the face, making her eyes sting and her nose run. She hated the simultaneous hot-cold feeling, hated that all it took was a simple thought of his pale blue eyes and quick smile to make her breath catch and her chest feel hollow.

Felicity managed to master her emotions before she arrived at Grape Seed Ranch and turned down the drive. The homestead was handsome, with a beautiful yard surrounding the house. She parked by the biggest barn and got out of her car, wondering where to go next.

"Mornin'," a man called, and Felicity turned, ready to pin her smile in place and make it through this day.

One day at a time, she coached herself. Her mom had told her that every day following Dad's death. Felicity had tried to stay at the family ranch. She really had.

She turned, thinking this ranch already felt better. Freer. Like the air held oxygen instead of pure sadness.

"You must be Felicity." The cowboy drew closer, and Felicity sucked in a breath when she recognized him.

He froze in the next nanosecond, obviously recognizing her too.

He was the cowboy she'd dunked with a single throw, after plenty of capable men hadn't been able to get the job done. And by the dark look filling his face, he wasn't happy to see her again.

CHAPTER TWO

"Yes, I'm Felicity Lightburne," she managed to say. She stepped forward and extended her hand to him.

"I'm Dwayne Carver." He took her hand, his fingers warm and wonderful against hers. He easily stood over six feet tall and sandy blond hair peeked out from under his cowboy hat. A different one from Friday night, Felicity noted.

"Sorry about the dunking," she added as he pumped her hand. Sparks traveled up her arm and popped through her shoulders. He pulled his hand away quickly and stuffed it in his pocket.

"You ruined a three-year record, I'll have you know." He sounded grumpy about it, and his bright blue eyes crackled with lightning. "And my best pair of boots."

She glanced at his footwear, which seemed just fine to her. "I played softball growing up." She didn't mention her father had coached her. It seemed like every thought in her mind contained the painful reminder of her dad, even here, miles and miles from where all the memories had been made.

"One ball." He shook his head, the hint of a smile pulling at his strong mouth. A twitter started in her stomach, one that chirped of his handsomeness, his chiseled features, his strong arms, and legs, and spirit.

Felicity tamed her thoughts and adjusted her hat on her head, certain the morning sun wasn't the only thing warming her. "So I was told I could board my horses here."

Dwayne glanced at her car, his eyes stalling there as he took in the bright red muscle car. "You drive that?"

"It's a mustang," she said with a little shrug.

He chuckled. "A mustang. Right. So you didn't bring 'em with that."

"No, my brother brought the horses when I moved here last week."

"Last week," he said softly. Then he perked up. "You're boarding?"

She nodded, almost wilting with his proximity. "Yep, boarding." Her voice scratched against her throat, but he didn't seem to notice.

"Let's go get 'em. You have a trailer?"

She met his eyes again, almost falling into their depths. Catching herself before she turned into pudding at this cowboy's second-hand boots, she said, "No trailer. Can't pull it with that." She smiled at her car. It had been good to her over the years.

"No, I don't suppose you can." He grinned too, making him so good-looking, it should be a crime.

"Where you livin'?" He took slow steps away from the parking area, and she went with him.

"Out near the Hammond peach orchards?" Why she phrased it as a question, she wasn't sure. "I'm renting a cottage on Bartlett Street."

"Yeah, I know the area." He cast her a quick smile and ducked his head. "So I'll hook up my trailer and we'll go get your horses. Then I can show you around the ranch and we can talk about what we need you to do here at Grape Seed."

He obviously wasn't the one who'd called and interviewed her. She'd remember his rich baritone voice, as it sent a bolt of heat straight through her. She needed to get a grip on her emotions before they stampeded her.

He's just another cowboy, she told herself as she followed him toward a four-bay garage. He'd either find her too masculine for his taste, as most of the other men she'd dated had. Or he'd treat her as just one of the guys, overlooking her femininity completely. She preferred both of those to the men who seemed cowed by her, and at least he hadn't done that.

She jumped in to help him hitch the trailer to the truck, and then she climbed into a new, nice vehicle. Black leather and the scent of oranges greeted her, and she realized that this ranch had a lot more money than the one she came from.

"All right," he said in that sexy-sweet drawl of his. "So you must have your horses over at Levi's."

"Yeah," she said. "How'd you know?"

"He's the only operation with horse boarding." He filled the seat next to her, his cologne like a siren's call to her. She hadn't come here to find a boyfriend. Hadn't even thought about dating a man in a few years now. She'd just needed somewhere that wasn't filled with memories of her father. Somewhere to find refuge from the storm her life had become without her dad in it.

But as Dwayne rumbled down the lane and then turned on the road and headed back to town, Felicity thought he might just be an added bonus to her move to Grape Seed Falls.

Say something, Dwayne told himself. Say something. Say something. Say something. He couldn't think of a single thing to say to the most beautiful woman he'd ever laid eyes on.

Finally he came up with, "So what brings you to Grape Seed Falls?"

"This job," she said, almost woodenly. He cut her a glance but didn't know her at all and couldn't tell if his question had annoyed her.

"My dad said you trained horses at a ranch near Dallas." His curiosity had always gotten him in trouble, but he couldn't help himself. He wanted to know everything about her, including how long she thought she'd be with the ranch.

"I did." Another two-word answer. Anxiety attacked him, making his leg muscles tight and the tremor in his right hand more pronounced. He'd trembled the teensiest bit while they were shaking hands too, but he'd pulled away quickly and hid his hand in his pocket. Felicity hadn't seemed to notice, something for which Dwayne was grateful.

"Who taught you how to train horses?"

"My dad." She folded her arms over her stomach, and Dwayne took it as a hint to stop asking questions. He gripped the steering wheel with his right hand to keep his infirmity dormant. At least Levi's farm was on the west side of town, same as the ranch, so the drive wouldn't take long.

They arrived in record time, and Dwayne almost leapt from the truck before he flipped it into park. His anxiety couldn't be caged sometimes, and at least he could release some of it into the wide sky above Levi's stables.

"They're down here." She nodded toward the pastures that bordered the entire east side of the property. "I've come to ride them before."

"Every day, I bet." He stepped to her side, wishing he could position himself on her right, which was ridiculous really. He wasn't going to hold her hand. But, if he did, he'd want to hold her right with his left so his tremors could stay secret for a while longer.

Might as well tell her, he thought. She'd find out soon enough. All the cowboys on the ranch knew, and he loved that he didn't have to hide it from anyone out there. He was more self-conscious when he went into town, held his hand in a fist in the grocery store, and sat with his right side against the wall when attending church.

Before he could say anything, Felicity made tiny clicking

sounds with her tongue, and two horses in the pasture lifted their heads and came toward her eagerly. They had similar markings for a pair of paint horses, though one boasted a darker shade of brown than the other. The smaller one arrived first, lifting her nose over the fence and accepting Felicity's touch.

He watched the woman and felt her love for her horses permeate the air. She seemed crisp around the edges, but possessed softness too. His own smile melted across his face as he gazed at her. With a start, he realized he was staring—and turning into a marshmallow just watching this woman interact with her horses.

"So what are their names?" he asked, reaching out to stroke the second horse as it arrived.

"That's Linus," she said. "He's getting old. This here's his younger sister, Lucy."

"Linus and Lucy," Dwayne repeated, happiness slipping through him. "Funny."

"The car is named Charlie Brown."

Dwayne tipped his head back and laughed. "So you're a real Peanuts fan."

"My father loved the Peanuts." Her demeanor changed as if a switch had been flipped, and Dwayne sensed the sadness in her.

"Loved?" he asked, unable to censor himself. "Does he like something different now?"

She shook her head, her throat working as she swallowed. She leaned forward and put her forehead against Lucy's. "He—he's—" She exhaled, a blush rushing into her face.

"It's fine," Dwayne said. "I'll go find Levi." He edged away from her, half-hoping she'd call him back. She didn't, and he gave her the space he sensed she needed.

He found Levi in the tack room of the front barn, and Dwayne admired the newer equipment, the airy space, the clean floors. His tack rooms out at Grape Seed Ranch definitely needed an upgrade.

"Morning, Levi," he said, causing the other man to turn.

"Dwayne." Confusion crossed the other man's face. "What brings you out here?"

"Felicity Lightburne has her horses here. We're moving them to my ranch. It's part of our agreement."

"Oh, right." Levi glanced out the window, but it didn't face the direction of the pastures. "She mentioned she'd be starting there soon."

"Today." He ran his fingers over the stitching on a saddle hanging on the wall. "Heard anything about the auction in Austin?"

Levi paused in his work and nodded, a knowing glint in his eye. "Yeah, Clarion Champions will be there. Rumor is they'll have six horses up for auction."

Dwayne's first love was horses, but Grape Seed Ranch was a cattle operation. He couldn't do everything required to keep eighteen thousand head of cattle cared for and alive and train horses. Thus, the addition of Felicity to the staff.

But Dwayne hoped he could learn from her—and the fact that she was beautiful had nothing to do with his desire to stick to her side and take notes of everything she did. No, it did not.

"Probably be expensive," Dwayne said, his thoughts spinning from Felicity to horses and back again.

Levi chuckled and went back to organizing his toolbox full of horseshoeing equipment. "No doubt. You gonna go see what they bring?"

"Definitely." Both men laughed, and peace settled in Dwayne's soul. Levi was just like him: A first son who'd taken over the family business, and they shared an unspoken friendship because of their choices.

He nodded out the window. "Looks like she's ready to go."

Dwayne leaned forward so he could see out the window too. Felicity passed in front of him, leading both horses with a set of reins. "Yeah, and I'm her ride." He sighed like it was a terrible thing to be.

"And her boss, right?" Levi jostled some tools, creating a metal-on-metal sound that grated against Dwayne's nerves. He could never be a farrier. Too many loud noises that sounded like explosions. Too much hot iron that reminded him of the scent of a bomb.

"She's my new trainer, yes." He reached up and pushed his hat lower on his head as if Levi would see the heat rising through his neck.

"She any good?"

"My father seemed to think so." Dwayne turned to leave the tack room so Felicity wouldn't wonder where he'd gone. "You can't steal her from us."

"I can try!" Levi called after him. "Especially if she's good!"

Dwayne chuckled, but his determination was set. Felicity was *his* horse trainer, and he wouldn't let her go without a fight. As he emerged into the bright sunlight, a thought struck him like lightning.

He was prepared to do almost anything to keep her at Grape Seed Ranch, and he hadn't even seen her work with a horse yet.

Inhaling deeply, he told himself to pull back on the reins. Just because she was pretty didn't mean she was interested in him. She clearly had something plaguing her, the same way he did.

He found himself offering a prayer on her behalf as he hurried over to the horse trailer and got it unlocked for her so she could load Linus and Lucy. They took some coaxing, but eventually she had them tied in and ready to roll.

"So." Dwayne took a moment to adjust the air conditioning once he'd climbed into the cab of the truck. "Breakfast?"

She whipped her head toward him so fast, a flash of pain stole across her face. She rubbed her neck and squinted at him. "Breakfast?"

"My mom'll have somethin' at the homestead we can eat." He flipped the truck into gear, cursing himself for making the meal sound like an invitation to dine with him alone. Wondering why the mistrust had entered Felicity's expression so quickly. Clenching his right fist to keep his tremors dormant just a little longer.

CHAPTER THREE

"Hey, Ma," Dwayne called as he entered the homestead, Felicity just a few steps behind him. They'd unloaded the horses into their own stalls, and they seemed content for now. With the truck and trailer back in the vehicle shed, Dwayne's stomach grumbled for something to eat.

And he needed a break from the beautiful woman trailing him around the ranch. He hadn't been out with anyone in years, and he wasn't sure if her small talk was meant to be polite or if she was genuinely trying to be friends with him. His brain hurt from spending a couple of hours with her, and his muscles screamed at him for a release. If he could introduce her to his parents, maybe his dad would take over the tour of the ranch.

But today, the homestead stood empty, without the scent of maple bacon, or pancakes, or even coffee.

"Huh." Dwayne stopped in the large kitchen and turned in a slow circle. "They're not even here."

"You don't know where they are?" She glanced around the comfortable house too.

"I'm sure they told me." Foolishness blipped through him. "I've got a lot on my mind most of the time." He pulled out his phone and sent a text to his mother, who might answer if she happened to be looking directly at her phone right this second.

He put the device on the counter and reached for the fridge, his hand shaking like crazy. He pulled in a breath and held it, but the tremors assaulted him now, and there was nothing to be done about them. "We had hot dogs and macaroni salad last night for dinner. Sounds like breakfast today, right?"

Felicity, who had yet to do much in the way of smiling or laughing, giggled. Dwayne paused in his extraction of the world's best macaroni salad and twisted to look at her. Her pink lips curved up, and a blush colored her cheeks, making her freckles more pronounced. She honestly was a vision from heaven.

"I don't think anyone eats hot dogs for breakfast," she said, shaking her head like he was a naughty three-year-old but she loved him anyway.

He shook out the traitorous L-word and pulled the bowl of macaroni salad from the fridge. "All right," he said. "But what about this? It's pasta, vegetables, and Italian dressing. It's practically an omelet." He opened the cupboard, but only took down one bowl at a time. Sometimes, when he was really shaking, he couldn't grip objects. And holding heavy things? Didn't happen.

He placed a bowl in front of her with, "I think you're really going to like this." As he started to pull his hand away so he could gather two forks, her fingers trailed over his wrist.

Seizing, he froze. Everything in him seemed encased in cement, from his lungs, to his feet, to his eyes as they watched her trace a path from his arm to his knuckles.

Her touch was warm, and welcome, and sent pulse after pulse of desire and heat through Dwayne's poor, dry, cold soul. He could only think, *What is going on here?*

FELICITY DIDN'T KNOW WHAT SHE WAS DOING. SHE WANTED TO

touch him, so she had. "Your hands...." She let her words fade into silence, because she couldn't say what she really wanted to.

Your hands are beautiful.

Why do they shake like that?

Are you nervous? Afraid?

Your hands are beautiful.

And he did have wonderful hands. Tan and large and strong, yet soft and comforting at the same time. She slid her fingers through his and pressed her palm to his. One squeeze, and she came to her senses.

"I'm so sorry," she whispered, dropping her hand and backing up a step. The scent of the Italian dressing filled her nose with a sharp, tangy smell that suddenly made her queasy. "I'll...." She fell back another step. "Maybe you can just show me what I should be doing."

Dwayne finally lifted his eyes to hers, and the wonder swimming in those gorgeous cerulean depths nearly unlatched the floodgate she kept locked on her emotions.

"My hands shake," he said, his voice no louder than hers had been. It seemed to fill the whole house though. "Well, just my right one."

Felicity couldn't help looking at it again. His fingers barely moved, but they definitely trembled the slightest bit. She hadn't noticed it until he'd reached for the bowls, and then everything in her had wanted to touch him.

She fisted her own fingers, surprised and horrified at her stupidity. On the job for two hours and she was holding hands with the boss?

Stupid, stupid, stupid, she scolded herself.

"Do you want to know why?" he asked.

She did, but she couldn't bring herself to say so. Or nod. So she shrugged. "I don't want to intrude. I'm really sorry I touched you. I shouldn't have—" She stopped talking when he lifted that beautiful, trembling hand in a silent attempt to quiet her.

"It's fine," he drawled, and she really liked the way he twanged out the word *fiiine*, almost like it was two syllables instead of one. He turned back to the pasta salad and used that damaged hand to pull a spoon and two forks from the utensil drawer. He scooped some macaroni into each of their bowls and started eating.

Just the thought of putting anything in her mouth made her squeamish.

"You're not hungry?" he asked.

"I'm—" *Embarrassed. Confused. Ready to get to work.* They would all fit. So would *Attracted to you in a way I haven't felt in a long, long time.*

Instead of finishing, she picked up her fork and took a bite of the salad, making sure to get a chunk of something green with the mouthful of noodles. Sweet and sour had a party in her mouth. She swallowed and said, "This is really good."

"World's best," he said proudly, a grin gracing his face and making her heart ripple like a flag in a stiff wind. "Its won best salad at the Grape Seed Falls Family Festival for three straight years now."

She smiled too, the gesture feeling nice on her face. She hadn't had reason to do a lot of smiling or laughing lately, and she'd done both today already. Felicity hadn't known why she needed to leave her father's ranch and come here. She'd only known it was the right thing to do.

Standing in a strange kitchen and eating macaroni salad with a handsome man shouldn't feel so right—or so scandalous. But it felt like both of those things, and Felicity couldn't help the second smile that slipped across her face.

ONLY THIRTY MINUTES LATER, EVERYTHING SHE'D EXPERIENCED in the kitchen—the wonder, the peace, the happiness—had faded to shock.

"There are *four* unbroken horses here?" She looked at Dwayne like he'd just pulled an April Fool's prank on her.

"I believe the ad said we needed someone immediately." He watched the wild horses with his mouth set in a grim line. She much preferred the flirty, fun grin. "Now you know why."

Four unbroken horses.

Unbelievable.

She usually worked with one horse at a time, as it was exhausting work to break and train a horse. Not only physically but mentally, emotionally, spiritually. She gave everything she had to the animal, and the patience required...well, she wasn't sure she could do it times four.

"And it's just me?" She disliked the squeaky quality of her voice on the last word.

His boots scuffed the concrete where they stood. "Well, I was hopin'...that is, I—I'd really like to learn how to break horses better." His words tumbled out of his mouth now. "You'll see that some of ours aren't that well behaved, and it's because I'm not the best horse whisperer out there."

Felicity frowned, unsure of everything and turned in a slow circle as she faced the stable. Their whole herd was rowdy? She closed her eyes and prayed for strength. "So I'm going to train you too, is that it?"

More boot scuffling, and Felicity's annoyance lifted another degree. "I don't have time to train the horses. That's why we have four unbroken, and a bit of a naughty herd."

"You don't have time." She wasn't sure why she was repeating his words. At least the stable seemed to be in decent repair, but she hadn't stepped foot inside quite yet. "Are you the foreman or something?"

"No, Kurt's the foreman."

"What are you so busy doing then?"

"I own the ranch. Well, I will, once my father retires. But he's essentially retired now. I do everything the owner does." He shot her a quick glance. Nothing long enough to grab and hold onto, see how he was feeling. Although, the defeated notes in his voice didn't fall on deaf ears.

"You own the ranch."

"It does decently well," he said, and she thought about the expensive vehicles in the shed. "But we need help with the horses." He leaned against the fence now, his gaze on the animals in the pasture. "They're great horses."

"You love horses." She wasn't asking. She could simply hear it in his voice, see it in his profile.

"Yeah."

"But you're too busy running a *cattle* ranch." She put one foot on the bottom rung and hoisted herself up so she was standing on the fence. A whistle through her teeth caught the attention of all four horses.

Only the black and white Tobiano spotted saddle horse lifted his head. She extended her hand toward him and said, "Come on."

The horse took a few hesitant steps toward her and stopped. He was gorgeous, standing at least sixteen hands tall. Felicity felt him burrowing into the soft part of her heart, and she knew they'd get along fine.

"I'll start with him. Does he have a name?"

"Spotlight."

She climbed down from the fence and leaned her back into it. "Okay, Dwayne. Here's the deal."

He looked at her, and a skitter of nerves raced through her, causing her pulse to pound against the back of her throat. "I'll start with Spotlight. You choose one you'll start with, and we'll train them together. I'll train Spotlight, and I'll train you how to train...."

"Payday," he said. "He's the Rocky Mountain chocolate out there."

She glanced over her shoulder to the horse who hadn't even responded to her whistle. "He's pretty."

"He's my favorite. I bought him only a month ago."

She grinned at him, pleased when he swallowed hard. "You make it a habit to buy horses and then leave them out to pasture?"

"I like buying horses," he admitted.

"And yet you own a cattle ranch."

"Duty," he said. "My brother left a long time ago. My sister teaches third grade. Someone has to run the ranch my parents spent their whole lives building."

She cocked her head and tried to absorb what he'd said. "But if you don't love it...."

"I *do* love it," he said. "I love this ranch. My men. Being away from the town. I just happen to love horses more than cows." He gave her another million-watt smile. "But the cows pay most of the bills, so I'm...dabbling in horses right now."

Felicity laughed, the sound rich and delicious as it bubbled from her throat. She couldn't remember the last time she'd laughed like that. It felt good. It cleansed something inside her that had been dark and sticky before.

"Dabbling in horses," she said. "All right." She turned back to the chocolate Rocky Mountain horse with the flaxen mane and tail, leaning into the fence mere inches from Dwayne. "Horse training is a full-time job. Who's gonna do what you normally would?"

"I will."

She nudged him with her shoulder playfully. The gesture felt easy, yet also a bit forced. She hadn't flirted with a man in a while. "So you're going to work twenty hours a day?"

He nudged her right back. "Whatever it takes."

Felicity liked his drive, his hard-working spirit, the scent of his cologne. She wondered about his tremor, and how he'd come to love horses more than cows, and if they could maybe be more than two people training horses together.

She pulled on the train of thought, trying to bring it back before it ran away. After all, she'd only met Dwayne—a man who collected wild horses like other people collected coins.

"Maybe you can teach me how to do whatever it is you do," she said.

"Like fixing fences and painting barns and repairing training rings?"

"Yeah, like that."

"So you'll be dabbling in ranching."

She'd like to think she'd be dabbling in Dwayne, but she just smiled and said, "Sure. Dabbling in ranching."

CHAPTER FOUR

D
wayne seemed uncomfortable inside his own barns, and he kept saying things like, "We're gonna get that tack room insulated," and "Don't worry about those fences. I'll get the boys to patch them up," and "This is the training ring, but we'll get it leveled before you start."

He flitted from one thing to the next like a hummingbird looking for the best nectar. His nervous energy floated like a scent on the air, and Felicity wanted to grab onto his shoulders and say, "Take a breath. It's okay."

But she couldn't reach his shoulders without some effort, and she liked walking around the ranch and just drinking in the atmosphere of it. Grape Seed was a bit different from the ranch where she'd grown up. They were larger, with nicer equipment, and a lot more money. Sure, her parents had done okay, and her two younger brothers planned to keep the ranch afloat.

That was about what they did—stay afloat.

Felicity had never minded, because she raised horses from foals and sold them once they were ready to be ridden.

"How many horses do you have here?" she asked Dwayne once he'd seemed to settle on one task—feeding his collection.

"Twenty-nine," he said immediately. "Some are working horses for the ranch. I guess that would be the goal for all our horses." He threw her a look over his shoulder.

"Not necessarily," she said. "Linus and Lucy aren't working horses."

"Right. We have thirty-one horses here now."

"Which one's yours?"

"They're all mine."

"No, which one's yours?"

Before he could answer, a dog zipped into the barn. His whole body wagged as he trotted over to Dwayne. "Hey, boy." He handed the hose to Felicity, and she held it in the trough while he scrubbed down the border collie.

"He's beautiful," she said as the dog licked Dwayne's face, causing him to laugh. The sound lit up Felicity's whole body. She imagined him laughing like that into the hollow of her neck, maybe whispering something sweet just before he kissed her....

"You're overflowing," he said, taking the hose from her and moving down the row.

She felt as if someone had ignited a stick of dynamite and tossed it down her throat. She could barely swallow and heat flamed in her face. Maybe if she doused herself with the hose, she'd figure out what was wrong with her.

Nothing's wrong, she told herself as she took the hose from Dwayne again. *He's attractive. Nothing wrong with being attracted to him.*

Though he was her boss, and she wasn't sure what to do with those feelings of attraction. She hadn't felt them for anyone in a while, and while she was still in Texas, she felt totally out of her element in this new town, on this new ranch, with all these new feelings.

So she focused on the one thing that wasn't new to her: taking care of horses.

Dwayne stayed in place beside Felicity when he should've moved away. He took the hose from her when she could've done the job herself. He thrilled at the way she sidled back up to him and took the hose from him again.

It was like they were dancing without touching. Without talking. Jinx had flopped in the corner of the barn, his tongue hanging out of his mouth. Usually Dwayne would talk to the border collie, ask him where Atlas was and if he'd seen any of the boys that morning for a bite of scrambled eggs or to play a quick game of fetch.

Of course, the dog never answered, but Dwayne had always felt less lonely if he had a dog to talk to.

"What's the dog's name?" Felicity asked.

"Jinx," he said. "And I have a German shepherd named Atlas. He's old, though. Probably snoozing in the shade under my porch." He forked hay into the feed bin, though there was no horse in the stall. He kept them out in the pastures during the summer, only opening the doors to the stables and barns at night.

"So you don't live with your parents?"

Dwayne thought he detected a note of interest, but he quickly dismissed the notion. Felicity was beautiful and capable, and she wouldn't be interested in a man like him. He let his eyes trace the curve of her hip before dropping his eyes to her sexy cowgirl boots. He'd never dated a cowgirl before—had never even thought of it.

Most of the women in town were pretend cowgirls, only wearing the boots and hats to the summer rodeos. But Felicity was the real deal, and Dwayne liked everything he'd seen and almost all of what he'd heard.

"No," he said. "There's a guest house on the edge of the homestead. It's two bedrooms and two baths. I've been livin' there for a while."

"How long's a while?"

"Oh, ten years now, I guess."

She handed him the hose as they'd reached the end of the line.

"And what do you do in your guest house?" She was definitely flirting with him now.

"You know," he said, coiling the hose as he went to hang it on the holder. "Make caramel popcorn and sit on the porch with my guitar."

She giggled, a pretty little sound that wormed its way into Dwayne's heart. "I didn't think you could play the guitar with sticky fingers."

"Sometimes I just hold it on my lap," he said. Anxiety punched him in the throat. Why had he said that? While it was true, he didn't want to explain the reasons why sometimes he rocked in his chair, the guitar dormant on his lap, as he stared across the land he owned and loved.

"Something else you're dabbling in?" she asked. Her dark eyes sparkled, reminding him of black onyx and diamonds.

"You could say that," he said. "Were you still living with your parents before you came here?"

She nodded, some of her fun and flirt fading. "We all worked the ranch together."

He noticed the past-tense verb again, but opted not to say anything this time. He nodded, and they finished the chores in the horse barn and the north stable.

"So, do you want to meet my horse?" he asked.

"Yeah. Yes, of course." She folded her arms and gazed up at him. The powerful need to lean down and taste her mouth almost brought him to his knees.

He swallowed and leaned back, trying to control his spiraling thoughts and emotions. "Don't laugh at the name, all right? I bought him in an auction about three years ago, and the name came with." He led her to the next stable over, which had a decent-sized pasture attached to it.

He gestured toward the horses clustered in the corner, all of them trying to stand in the bit of shade cast by the building. "The black and white one. See how his hooves look like they've been dipped in white paint? That's Gaston."

She half-snorted, half-scoffed, but when he cast her a quick look, she sobered.

"I didn't name him, remember?" He extended his hand over the fence, and Gaston came toward him, thankfully.

The last thing he needed was for his personal horse to behave badly in front of the expert horse trainer.

"But I think his name fits." He stroked the horse's cheeks, feeling a new measure of peace infuse his soul. Horses always helped him emotionally, especially after he'd come home from the Marines, which was why he felt such a draw to them.

"He's proud," he continued when Felicity didn't say anything. "A bit stubborn. Thinks he's the cream of the crop, like all the ladies want him. Then he just hangs out with all these other male horses." He chuckled like his horse's behavior was truly unique.

"Gaston." She reached up and let the horse see her hand before touching his head. Dwayne noted the way she watched the horse, almost trying to size it up before making a judgment. "You're a handsome horse."

Gladness filled Dwayne's heart. For some reason, it was important to him that Felicity like his horse.

"How old are you?" he asked. "Youngest in your family? Oldest?"

"I'm the oldest. Two younger brothers still back on the ranch."

"I'm oldest too," he said. "Thirty-three."

"Thirty-two." She shared a smile with him, and his heart dang near exploded out of his chest. "So we'll start tomorrow with Spotlight and Payday. Deal?"

"Deal." Dwayne enjoyed a few more minutes with her, then she made her good-byes and headed for that shiny red sports car. He'd never considered owning a car like that—number one, it was too low to the ground. He would never be able to fold his tall frame inside. And getting out was worse.

But Felicity ducked into the car and the roar of a really big engine filled the air a moment later. It was a beautiful mustang, carrying a lovely woman, even if it wasn't the type of mustang he was used to.

He went about the rest of his day, his thoughts never far from Felicity. As he strolled over to the Cowboy Commons, as Kurt liked to call the row of cabins that flanked the road on the east side, he wondered if he'd be up to the task of training a horse the way she did.

The cabins came into view. Eight of them in all, four on each side of the road, made up the Commons. He and Kurt had repainted them all the color of dark chocolate three years ago, and each cowboy chose the color for their front door. Dwayne's father had bought whatever colors the boys wanted, and Dwayne passed cherry red, and mint green, and butter yellow.

Each cowboy got their own cabin, and there was a picnic area complete with a flagpole, as if these eight houses had formed a community. The foreman had a slightly larger cabin on the other side of the picnic area, an addition to the ranch his father had put in after a few years of owning Grape Seed Ranch. He was still part of the community, though he was offset just a bit. Dwayne was not, so far removed from this part of the ranch and being the boss.

He got along great with the men, sure. They liked him and respected him. Because Dwayne yearned to be part of something like their community, he came out to the Cowboy Commons often. It had become something and somewhere where he could be himself and belong.

The dust finally settled after Felicity's departure, and he wondered if she could be the one he belonged to. Belonged *with*.

"There you are," Kurt said, his voice on the upper edges of panic as he appeared around the side of his cabin. His chest heaved and he took one, two, three big breaths. "We need you in the bullpens. Tiger's demolished the north fence, and all the bulls are out."

He didn't wait for Dwayne to confirm. Kurt turned and headed back the way he'd come.

Dwayne's feet slipped a little in the old cowboy boots he hadn't worn in months. But he got them moving after Kurt, his heartbeat galloping as fast as he knew his stubborn bulls were.

CHAPTER FIVE

Dwayne saddled Gaston faster than he ever had. He found Kurt atop a sorrel-colored horse, practically pacing as he waited. "Let's go," Dwayne said.

They rode out to the bullpens, which sat on the far west side of the ranch. The same side as his mother's rose gardens, the peach and apple trees, and her vegetable garden. As early as it was in the growing season, she didn't have much Tiger would want.

But Dwayne knew he'd find the bull out there, stomping through what she worked to keep beautiful, searching for something to satisfy his sweet tooth.

"Did you get an apple?" he called to Kurt.

"We've tried that. He's not comin' in this time."

Dwayne set his mouth into a tight line and urged Gaston to go faster. They arrived on the west side of the house only to see everything in order. Well, not quite. Evidence that Tiger had been here, rooting for a sweet carrot or a handful of strawberries, was obvious in the torn up ground.

"Where is he?"

The radio on Kurt's hip beeped, and Austin's voice came on, saying, "He's headed for the south road."

And the south road led to town. Tiger was a regular Houdini, always trying to escape the confines of his pen. He usually just wanted a treat, but this felt like a deliberate attempt to let Dwayne know that he wasn't happy with all the fences.

Dwayne knew how he felt. But fences kept things neat, and carrots in the ground, and bulls from goring townspeople.

"Call the Sheriff," he called to Kurt, who managed to pull his cell phone from his back pocket while keeping his horse at a gallop. A flash of emotion struck Dwayne. He wasn't sure if it was jealousy or inadequacy. Probably both. Because he couldn't make a call and control a horse at the same time. Not since the explosion in Iraq.

He also hadn't ridden this aggressively in a while, and combined with the time he'd spent on the board over the water in the dunk tank, and his bones felt like they were knocking together with every stride Gaston took.

A line of horses appeared ahead, and it took a moment for Dwayne to realize they were his cowboys. All stopped. The horses sidestepped and pawed the ground, as if nervous.

What in the world?

His heart dropped to his stirrups. Tiger had hurt someone.

But why weren't his boys doing anything?

Please, God, he thought. *Please help us get this bull contained without injury.*

He pulled up at the end of the line, the last to arrive and hating that fact. As the owner, he should be the first on any scene. He should know what to do. His father would've been first. His dad would know what to do.

As Dwayne sucked in breath after breath, he couldn't make sense of what he saw before him. Maybe his dad wouldn't know what to do in this situation.

Tiger, the brownish-black bull with a white face, stood with his rump toward the line of cowboys. Three other bulls stood slightly behind Tiger, and though they weren't as large, they certainly made a terrifying line no one should cross.

In a face-down with the four bulls was a red mustang. Not the horse. The car.

With Felicity behind the wheel.

Dwayne's throat felt like someone had scrubbed it out with sandpaper and then lit it on fire. Men asked him questions. The radio on Austin's hip bleeped. Kurt's cell phone blared out its obnoxious ringtone. Jinx barked and barked, circling the bulls without tightening the radius, as if even he could sense something dangerous was about to happen.

Dwayne didn't have time to wonder what she was doing, coming back to the ranch instead of heading away from it.

He needed to diffuse those bulls before they charged.

FELICITY GRIPPED THE STEERING WHEEL. THE CAR, THOUGH made of steel, didn't feel like adequate protection against the eight thousand pounds of angry bull standing in front of her. The all-black animal on her right had saliva dripping from its jowls, and the biggest one lowered its head as if it was about to charge.

The car was already in reverse, but she kept her foot jammed on the brake. Number one, she wasn't great at backing up without looking behind her. Number two, she couldn't look away from the four pairs of bovine eyes staring at her.

Though her windows remained up, the barking from Dwayne's dog was plain to hear. He kept moving around the bulls, as if daring them to make one false move. Jinx switched his track to a back-and-forth motion between her car and the bulls at the same time Dwayne separated himself from the line of cowboys waiting a healthy distance away.

He directed Gaston to her left, giving the bulls a wide berth. One by one, the other cowboys moved out too, all going to the left or right and creating a circle around her car and the bulls. Somehow she tracked them without looking away from the angry animals in front of her.

She cracked the window half an inch, and the volume of the barking increased. A second dog arrived, a beautiful German shepherd who didn't seem like he spent his days snoozing in the shade.

He bared his teeth and barked, barked, barked.

"Back 'em up, Atlas," Dwayne called, his voice calm and tense at the same time.

Atlas snapped his teeth and lunged forward. The big bull took one step back. As if dog and bull had perfected a dance over the years, Atlas barked and snapped, lunged and flattened his body to the ground, and the bulls backed up a step at a time.

Red and blue lights flashed in her rearview mirror, but she only glanced at the Sheriff's SUV for a moment before refocusing on the situation in front of her.

Her ankle throbbed, and she just wanted to get out of here so she didn't have to tell Dwayne what had happened. He positioned his horse right in front of her hood, blocking her view. Frustration and fear combined into a firestorm, and she leaned to the side to keep her eyes on the four tons of bull-flesh.

Bulls aren't horses, she told herself, something she should've done before she'd started this stare-down. Even the Sheriff was smart enough to stay in his truck, and he'd obviously come to help.

Dwayne waved his hand, a clear indication that she should start backing up. She eased her foot off the brake pedal and let the car's fuel injection do its job. Inch by precious inch, she put more and more distance between her and Dwayne, between her and the bulls.

The dogs kept barking. The cowboys tightened in, making a line that now faced the bulls. They didn't have a windshield, or metal, or anything to get them out of harm's way, and her admiration for the ten men on horseback grew.

"Please help them," she prayed.

Jinx's barks intensified, and a sharp, canine yelp filled the air in the next moment. She reached for the door handle but stilled before repeating her stupidity.

Men yelled, and the Sheriff leapt from his car, his mouth moving fast as he spoke into his handheld radio.

That huge brown-black bull broke through the line, sending one cowboy flying from the saddle as he did.

"Dwayne!" she called, her fingers fumbling along the door latch despite her brain's insistence she *stay in the car!*

She was barely aware of the shouting around her as she rushed to the fallen form of the cowboy she'd been fantasizing about since dunking him. Reaching him, she knelt and let her hands hover above his torso. "What hurts?"

He groaned, twisting as pain crossed his face.

"Paramedics are on their way." The Sheriff arrived and crouched down. "Anything broken, Dwayne?"

"I don't think so," he said, his voice low and tired and filled with agony. Something was definitely hurt.

"Twenty minutes until they get here," the Sheriff said.

"Twenty minutes?" Felicity asked, glancing up. "Why so long?"

"Coming from—" Dwayne tried to sit up and collapsed back to the ground. "Crawford." He panted, favoring his right shoulder. His hand vibrated like hummingbird wings.

Pure guilt pulled through Felicity. She opened her mouth to apologize, to tell him that she'd gotten out of her car to soothe the bulls.

A scoff combined with part of a sob. *Soothe the bulls.* Honestly, what had she been thinking?

At least she'd made it back to her car without getting gored. But now Dwayne had gotten hurt.

"I'm sorry," she said, slipping her fingers through his trembling ones. She held on with both of her hands, willing him to understand that she hadn't meant to further enrage the bull, would never hurt him.

"Not your fault," he said, his voice strengthening with each word. He squeezed her hand back.

But it was her fault.

She glanced up when someone shouted, and the Sheriff shot to his feet. "They've got two of the bulls contained," he said. "That Tiger just won't go, will he?"

"He'll tire out eventually," Dwayne said. He shifted and moaned. "Felicity, can you—will you—?" He lifted himself up slightly, rolling partially away from her.

She edged closer to him and he rested his injured shoulder on her knees.

A sigh hissed from his mouth. "Thank you."

"Is it your ribs?" Felicity was about as far from a doctor as she could get, but she knew ribs took a long time to heal.

"No," he said. "My shoulder. It's been injured before." The tremors in his hand started to quiet.

"Get thrown off a horse?"

Atlas approached, his tail tucked between his legs. He nosed Dwayne, a whine in the back of his throat.

"I'm okay, boy." Dwayne reached up and scrubbed the dog's head. "You okay?"

The German shepherd sat down right next to Dwayne's chest and looked at Felicity as if he knew she was the cause of his master's injury. His tongue seemed to be a mile long, and the heat from his breath brushed her fingers.

"Atlas and I used to work together," Dwayne said.

"Oh yeah? Does he dabble in horses too?"

"Explosives," Dwayne said. "He can sniff 'em out better than any other dog." He grinned at the dog, and the gesture was so sweet and sincere that Felicity's heart melted. "Can't you, boy?"

"You worked around explosives?" Her voice sounded almost like a whisper, filled with reverence. She wanted to know, but she didn't want to pry.

"I was a Marine corporal, and he was a military combat dog. We worked together." Dwayne closed his eyes, and sirens went off in Felicity's head.

"Hey, stay awake, okay?" She stroked her fingers across his brow line and tried not to drink in handsomeness.

His eyes opened again, and they looked right at each other.

"I'm so sorry," she said. "I was just coming back to feed Linus and Lucy, and there were bulls out, and I thought I could...."

He reached up with his left hand and brushed her hair off her face. "It's not your fault. Tiger busts through the fence a couple times a year."

She bit back the rest of her confession—the part where she got out of her car and actually walked toward a one-ton animal as if her presence alone could calm it. She nodded. "They should be here soon."

She willed the ambulance driver to go faster and prayed that Dwayne would be just fine.

CHAPTER SIX

By the time Felicity limped into her dark cottage on Bartlett Street, it was just past midnight. And for someone who rose before the sun, that equaled pure exhaustion. She'd refused to leave Dwayne's side until his parents and sister had arrived at the hospital. She'd met them all and then retreated to the waiting room, where she'd sat with Kurt.

The foreman had reported that the fences surrounding the bull pens had been fixed, and all the bulls were back where they belonged.

Dwayne had a separated shoulder and he'd been sent home. She'd left at the same time as him, and he'd smiled and waved with his left hand. She was sure she'd find him in the stable in the morning, and a sick feeling squirmed in her stomach.

She filled a teapot with water and set it on the stove. As far as she was concerned, there was nothing that couldn't be cured with chamomile. Well, except maybe the way she missed her father. Chamomile hadn't seemed to dull that ache any.

She changed out of her jeans and into a soft pair of pajamas. "Whiskers?" she called. The white cat mewed and came out from underneath the bed.

"Did you eat dinner?" Felicity scooped the cat into her arms and took her into the kitchen, where her food bowl sat partially empty. "Oh, you've got lots. Sorry I was gone so long today."

She jabbered to the cat as she made toast and gathered painkillers to go with her tea. After Whiskers knew all about Dwayne and the escaped bulls, after the toast was gone and the pills swallowed and the tea cold, Felicity finally collapsed into bed.

She supposed sleep would claim her immediately, as late as it was. But she started into the darkness and said, "Thank you for making Dwayne's injury minor."

She hadn't spent much time since her father's death conversing with the Lord. It seemed as though the ease with which she used to be able to express herself to Him had been erased. Blocked, almost.

She'd begged for so long for her father to get well, and He hadn't been listening then. But for the first time in months, she felt like maybe He was there, listening to her again.

———

Dwayne's shoulder woke him in the night with a dull ache. He got up and swallowed a couple of pills in the dark, stumbling over Atlas on his way back to bed. The dog jumped up and curled into Dwayne's side, a sigh ruffling his hair.

"I'm okay," he whispered to the dog who had been with him through some of the hardest days of his life. Though the relentless summers in Iraq, Atlas had never lost focus when it was over a hundred degrees and the tension was so thick in the air it was hard for Dwayne to breathe.

Atlas nosed Dwayne as if to say *Are you really okay?* As if the dog knew Dwayne had a storm brewing in his chest. Mostly from embarrassment at having been injured in front of all his cowboys. In front of Felicity.

But better him than any of them.

And it was only a separated shoulder. He'd be fine in a week or so. He'd known immediately what had happened, because this particular shoulder had been injured in the past. It hadn't needed surgery then, and it wasn't bad enough to warrant it this time either. Thankfully.

He dozed, only waking when Jinx started barking. Dwayne shot into a sitting position, sure that pesky bull had gotten out again. His front door opened a moment later, and his mom's voice filtered down the hall as she said, "Quiet, Jinxy. You'll wake Dwayne."

"I'm awake," he called, shoving in vain against Atlas, who hadn't seemed to notice the yapping of the other dog or the tapping of his mom's footsteps as she came closer.

"How'd you sleep?" She leaned in the doorway with concern etched around her eyes.

"Just fine," he said. No reason to alarm her. His letters home had been the same way. *Things are fine. Atlas is doing a great job. No danger here.*

Things usually were fine. Atlas did do a great job. But there was danger everywhere in Iraq.

"What are you doin' here?" he asked as he slid to the edge of the bed and stood.

"Thought I'd make you breakfast."

"I don't need you to do that."

"I know you don't." She turned and headed into his kitchen anyway. A few bangs later, and the sound of running water met his ears. He slowly lifted his right hand above his head, waiting for the scream of pain from his body that would alert him to stop. It didn't come.

A mild ache, and nothing more. Dwayne thanked the Lord for that, swallowed two more painkillers, and joined his mom in the kitchen. The scent of coffee and browning bread greeted him, and maybe he did like that his mother had come to take care of him for this one meal.

"Thatcher called," she said.

"Oh yeah?"

"He said he can come help if you need it."

"I'm fine," Dwayne said. "He doesn't need to come." He ran a veterinary clinic in Austin, and though it was only eighty miles away, Dwayne knew it wouldn't be easy for his brother to come. What would he do, anyway? He didn't know how to fix fences or repair harvesters or anything they did on the ranch.

But it was nice of him to offer, and Dwayne said as much.

"Daddy wants to know if you need him on the ranch today."

"No," Dwayne said. "You guys have your fishing trip, and I already ruined that." They'd gone up to Perdenales Falls State Park yesterday, as planned. Dwayne had just forgotten. They'd come home as soon as Kurt had called them, as it was less than an hour away.

"You didn't ruin anything," his mother said. "If you're really okay, we'll head back up there. We left the canoes and the boat."

"I'm really okay."

She set a plate of scrambled eggs and toast in front of him, and he grinned at her. "Thanks, Mom."

She ruffled his hair the same way she had when he was growing up, and a flash of gratitude for his parents zipped through him.

"Where is Dad?" he asked as she poured his coffee and he reached for the sugar bowl.

"Oh, you know Daddy. He went out to check the herd."

"We have men to do that."

"He can't help himself." She giggled and sat on the barstool next to him, a single piece of toast in her hand. "How was the new trainer?"

Dwayne almost choked on his bite of eggs. He swallowed, said, "Fine," and stuffed his mouth full again. They hadn't really done much yesterday, and he wasn't about to let something as silly as a separated shoulder keep him out of the training ring. "We're startin' today. She's going to teach me as she breaks Spotlight."

His mom watched him with her keen eyes, almost like she could tell he'd been attracted to Felicity.

"What?" he asked.

"I'm glad you've finally gotten your horse trainer is all." She grinned at him, her green eyes crinkling along the edges. His mother had always supported her kids' dreams, even when Thatcher had left for college and said he wasn't coming back. Even when Dwayne had told his parents he was more interested in horses than cows. Even when Heather had expressed interest in living in an area more surrounded by people.

His mom had raised them all, and she'd taught them to be kind and hardworking and good. Ranching only ran in Dwayne's blood, but that was enough. He hoped to have a son or a daughter one day who felt the same way, if only to keep this ranch his parents had cultivated for the past thirty-five years in the family.

"Thanks, Mom."

"When we get back from Perdenales Falls, you'll have to introduce us." She spoke like Dwayne had gotten engaged and hadn't brought the woman home to meet his parents yet. Before he could figure out how to respond, his mom stood and headed toward the front door. "See you this weekend."

"Bye," he said absently, wondering if his feelings for Felicity had really been so transparent. He wasn't even sure what those feelings were. How could his mom know about them already? And if she did, who else had seen the evidence of his attraction to the horse trainer?

"Oh, good morning, Kurt."

Dwayne turned as his mother side-stepped the foreman and left. Kurt filled the doorway, causing Dwayne to sigh. "I'm fine," he called toward the other cowboy.

"I was just comin' to check on you."

"You and everyone else."

Kurt chuckled as he closed the door behind him. "I take it your mom made breakfast." He moved into the kitchen and poured himself a cup of coffee.

"Don't drink that. We're not staying here." Dwayne stood and collected his cowboy hat from the end table in the living room. "We're late."

"Late for what?" Kurt brought his coffee mug with him despite Dwayne's foul look.

"I want to level the training ring this morning, before Felicity shows up." He reached for the doorknob and stepped out onto the front porch.

Kurt snorted and joined him at the railing. "It's not even seven-thirty yet."

"And the boys are probably done with the feeding already."

Kurt gazed into the brand new Texas day. "Probably."

"Good, get four of them over to the training ring. Felicity and I are starting there today, and it needs to be ready."

Kurt gave him a curious look and took another sip of coffee. "You'll be training a horse?"

"Apparently having four unbroken horses is a crime," he said. "And I want to learn how to be a better breaker." He lifted his uninjured shoulder into a shrug. "She said she'd help me, and we get the horses broken twice as fast."

A smile pulled at the corners of Kurt's mouth. "Oh, I'm sure she'll help you."

"What does that mean?"

"She's a pretty woman."

"So what?"

"So nothing." Kurt set his mug on the railing and started for the stairs. "We better get that ring leveled. I'll meet you over there." He walked away, leaving Dwayne to stew on what he'd said.

She's a pretty woman.

Of course other men would find her attractive. Dwayne just hadn't thought he'd have to compete with any of them. Didn't want to compete for Felicity's attention, her approval, her affections.

"Be the boss, then," he muttered to himself. Then he collected Kurt's coffee mug and took it inside the house, as if he were the man's maid or his mother.

SWEAT RAN DOWN THE SIDE OF HIS FACE AS HE SWEPT THE RAKE over the dirt. With four men, plus Kurt and Dwayne, the leveling in the training ring had only taken a couple of hours. The sun still shone like it had a personal vendetta against Grape Seed Falls, though, and Dwayne swiped off his hat and wiped his forehead.

"Water break," he called, noticing how red Shane's face was. A collective sigh rose into the air, and all the men moved out of the direct sunlight and into the shady barn next door. Kurt handed out water bottles and everyone drank.

"Who are you startin' with?" Gabe asked.

"Payday," Dwayne said.

"Hoo, boy," Kurt said. "He'll be a tough one to break."

Payday hadn't been at the ranch long, so though Dwayne had tried to break him, he hadn't gotten very far. Equipment needed to be repaired, and fields planted, and cattle moved. The horse had been put out to pasture, and a pin of guilt pushed into his heart. Maybe he shouldn't be buying horses he didn't have time to break. Maybe he shouldn't be planning to attend the auction in Austin, even though Clarion Champions was going to be there.

Still, the idea of missing out on a great horse made his gut writhe. So he'd just go and see. Didn't mean he had to buy a horse. Though, he'd never been to an auction where he didn't walk away with at least one horse....

He pushed the thought away as the distinct sound of a well-tuned engine filled the air. "Felicity's here," he said, tossing his empty water bottle in the trashcan and heading toward the exit.

Sure enough, her red mustang pulled into a parking space and she unfolded herself from behind the wheel. She wore a dark-wash pair of jeans today, a short-sleeved shirt the color of the bluebonnets that grew across the lane, and that black cowgirl hat. Today, though, she'd put on an indigo hatband to match her shirt.

She swung her gaze across the ranch, sweeping from left to right, before she turned and found him loitering in the doorway of the barn.

Dwayne's breath lodged somewhere behind his lungs. His brain screamed at him to breathe as she walked toward him. He found a limp in her stride, though she was definitely trying to hide it.

"Hey," he said, finally remembering how to inhale.

"How are you this morning?" She stopped several paces away and tucked her hands in her back pockets.

"Just fine."

"Oh, I brought you something." She turned back, her dark ponytail swinging with the movement. She retrieved something— the way she favored her left leg was obvious to him—from the mustang and approached him again. She came nearer, and nearer, until he could smell the sweetness of her perfume and see the laugh lines around her eyes.

"I'm not the best baker, and it's the first time I've used the oven in my cottage, but it's my mom's recipe." She held out a loaf of bread. "It's banana chocolate chip."

He took it, his fingers itching to touch hers. "You bake?"

Apprehension filled her eyes. "Don't be impressed." Her features softened as her worry melted away. "In fact, I wouldn't eat that without butter. And probably a lot of milk nearby. Or coffee. It's probably really dry."

Dwayne started peeling back the plastic wrap, releasing a sweet, banana scent that made his stomach grumble. "Smells good." He lifted the bread to his lips and took a big bite, right there in front of her.

Her eyes widened and then she tipped her chin toward the sky and laughed. And laughed.

Dwayne could barely chew, as he was trying to keep his own chuckles contained. He managed to swallow, say, "Not bad," and then he joined his joy to hers.

CHAPTER SEVEN

"I can't believe you gnawed on it like a bear," she said, still giggling.

Dwayne stuck the last piece of bread in his mouth, having eaten it as he showed her the newly leveled training ring. "I didn't gnaw on it like a bear," he said. "I took a bite. And it was good, as you can see I've just finished it."

She shook her head, her smile wonderful and warm and everything worth having. Dwayne wanted to make her laugh and smile every day for the rest of her life.

"So, why are you limping?" he asked.

Her head whipped up. "I'm not limping."

He rolled his eyes and held up his right hand, which clearly trembled. "And my hand doesn't shake."

Fire entered her dark eyes, only exciting Dwayne further. "Fine. I twisted my ankle yesterday."

"When did that happen?"

Her jaw jutted forward. "I'm fine."

"I know you are." He made his voice as soft as possible. "I'm just wondering when you got hurt. I didn't think anyone else had gotten injured."

Something fearful passed through her eyes. "Remember when I told you I thought I could tame the bulls?"

Dwayne cocked his head, searching his memory for that conversation. "No," he said slowly.

She sighed, and her shoulders visibly deflated. "I guess I didn't tell you." Felicity kept her gaze on the ground as she said, "I was coming back to feed Linus and Lucy, and I saw the bulls. For some reason—" She cleared her throat and backed up a step.

Dwayne took a step forward to keep their proximity close. "Yeah?"

"For some reason, I thought I could calm them. Get them back where they belonged."

"Alone?"

"And without a horse, or a rope." Her voice carried notes of sorrow, agony, shame.

Dwayne reached out and put two fingers under her chin, gently lifting her face until she looked at him. Sparks shot between them, and he knew then that the attraction he felt for her wasn't one-sided.

"How did you get hurt?" he whispered.

"I obviously couldn't soothe that bull. When I figured that out, I ran back to my car—"

"You were out of the car?" Horror bolted through him.

She nodded, her mouth drooping a little. "It's my fault you got hurt. I'm so sorry."

His fingers drifted down her neck, drinking in the softness of her skin. He brushed her shoulder and then let his hand drop. "It's not your fault."

"I certainly didn't calm anything down."

"You didn't make Tiger get out of the pen. You didn't make him charge."

Felicity's eyes seemed too glassy to Dwayne, and he really hoped she wouldn't cry. He didn't need to carry that around with him. His humiliation was heavy enough.

The moment between them lengthened and strengthened,

until Dwayne thought maybe he could carry around her sorrows, her griefs, her burdens. Would she help him shoulder his?

With his thoughts running rampant, the way Tiger had yesterday, he forced himself back a step. "I'm glad you're okay." He pushed his cowboy hat lower over his eyes and put more distance between them. "Should we get started with the horses?"

"Yes," she said, and her voice sounded strong, no tears in sight.

Dwayne breathed a sigh of relief—at least until she opened the gate to the pasture where the wild horses were kept and walked right in.

"Whoa. What are you doing?" Dwayne's hand landed on her lower arm and gripped.

Fire flamed through Felicity, same as it had when his skin had touched hers the last time. A shiver erupted down her spine at the ghost of his fingertips along her neck, her collarbone, her shoulder. This hold was just as thrilling, just as pulse-pounding.

"Getting the horses." She managed not to sound like a leaky balloon when she spoke. How, she didn't know.

"You don't even have a rope. Or a saddle. Or anything."

She looked at him, realizing that he really had no idea how to start training a horse. "We don't need ropes or saddles right now."

He glanced over his shoulder to the training ring, and Felicity followed his gaze. It looked different somehow, but she couldn't put her finger on what had changed. She squinted and frowned, then understanding hit her.

"The ring's been leveled," she said, switching her gaze to him. "Did you do that?"

"Yes." He clipped the word out between narrow lips.

"We might not use it for a few more days," she said as gratitude and warmth flowed through her. Here was Dwayne, injured, and yet he'd spent at least a few hours this morning getting the training ring ready. For her. He'd spent his precious time getting something ready *for her*.

She definitely hadn't invented the lightning between them, nor had she missed the way he'd stepped back carefully as confusion and desire warred in his expression. Felicity felt the same things battling each other inside her heart and mind too, so she couldn't fault him.

"Right now," she said, stepping slowly. "We just want the horses to get comfortable with us in their space. We control who comes and goes, not them. We'll go to them first, but they have to learn to come to us whenever we want them to."

She moved through the wild grass, glad when Dwayne came with her, positioning himself on her right side. "So how did you start with their training?"

"Oh, you know." He didn't look at her, but kept his eyes steadfastly on the four horses who'd clumped together in the shade of the barn.

"No, I don't know," Felicity said.

"Well." He exhaled like he needed to prepare for a long day of boring activity. "I'd make 'em walk behind me. Have them get used to the reins, the saddle, the bit. That kind of stuff."

She nodded. It wasn't bad training. Just not the order she went in. "A well-trained horse should *want* to be with you," she said. "Unless there's a really great patch of clover nearby, or a cowboy with a hay cube in his pocket." She smiled as she thought about her childhood horse, Cornflower.

"I had this beautiful mare when I was a little girl," she said. "My dad named her Cornflower, because she was so white she sometimes seemed to have a purple fringe around her." Felicity almost stumbled when she realized she'd vocalized a memory about her father and hadn't felt the crushing blow of sadness that always seemed to be one breath away.

She smiled and continued. "That horse would follow me anywhere." She giggled and tossed her ponytail over her shoulder. "Except if my father was around. Somehow she knew he had the access to the treats, and she was such a glutton. When I got frustrated that she seemed so enamored with a simple hay cube, he told me to put one in my pocket."

Felicity slid her hand in her pocket now, but of course she didn't find a hay cube. "Way down deep," she said. "And to never give it to her until we were done for the day. So I started doing that. Carried one of those silly cubes with me everywhere I went. And that Cornflower, she was right with me, all the time."

She removed her hand from her pocket and Dwayne's hand brushed against it, too precise to be casual. Felicity sucked in a breath, and on the next step, he captured her fingers in his.

"Anyway." Her voice came out higher than normal, and her heart thundered in her chest like the sky was about to split open. She hadn't held hands with a man in a while, and certainly not someone like Dwayne. He seemed so different, and yet so much like, the other cowboys she'd dated.

"After a while, I forgot about the hay cube. I stopped giving it to Cornflower after we were done training, or done working, or done riding. I stopped putting one in my pocket. And she still came with me everywhere I went."

They stepped, only the slight breeze rustling between them. His hand was so warm, and so large, and Felicity felt herself drop her guard another notch. She wanted to let him in, allow him to experience some of her life with her.

"So she learned her duty," Dwayne said.

"Yeah," Felicity said. "I guess she did."

"It's like what we do as humans," Dwayne said. "In the beginning, we're motivated by the prize at the end of the day. A paycheck for the work. A good feeling for serving someone. Doing what our mothers ask us to do. Something like that. We do our tasks out of duty." He paused, and she let his words roll around in her mind, trying to make sense of them.

"Then, after a while, those things become habits. They become part of us. Then we do the job, or serve our neighbors, or eat our vegetables, not because we feel obligated to, or because we're going to get a hay cube if we do it. We do it because we *want* to do it."

Felicity paused and peered up at Dwayne. She could see his handsomeness. His kind spirit. Even his determination and drive. All of it was there, right on his face and in his countenance for anyone to see. But she hadn't expected this quiet, powerful soul who spoke so philosophically. Who said things that resonated in her entire being—the way her father had.

"I think my father would've liked you," she finally said, feeling his presence near. She tried to grasp onto it, make him stay, bask in the comfort he'd always lent her. Her heartbeat bobbed and bounced as the feeling dissipated into the hot, humid Texas air.

"I'm sure I would've liked him too," Dwayne said, squeezing her hand and continuing toward the wild horses.

A sense of loss rolled over her, but that dismal sadness didn't descend the way it had in the past. She glanced up into the sky and drew in a deep breath filled with the scent of grass, and horses, and Dwayne's intoxicating cologne. A part of her that had felt forever shrouded in darkness lightened, and a smile touched her lips.

Thank you, she thought, unsure of why she'd thought it was God who had granted her this reprieve from the weight of her grief. In the past, she'd known of His goodness, His mercy, His grace.

Maybe now she needed to do what her father had always counseled her to do. When it doubt, try to believe until the doubts can be dismissed.

She cleared her mind and stopped walking now that the horses were within several paces. The big Tobiano spotted horse lifted his head, a wary look in his eye. The Rocky Mountain horse tossed his head, and Felicity held very still. The other two horses—a beautiful paint horse with precise markings and a bay with a glorious black tail and mane. She could see why Dwayne had bought these animals. They were stunning specimens of their breeds, and her appreciation for horses—*and for Dwayne?*—swelled within her heart.

She released his hand, and her head cleared a bit. Giving herself a bit of room to work, she clicked her tongue at the Tobiano. "Come on, Spotlight," she said, her voice not sweet or sugary, not condescending or coddling. Her father had taught her to talk like she normally did, and expect the horse to come to her.

Still, it surprised her every time one of them did.

Felicity caged her fear and stuffed it as far from her as possible. Horses could sense such things, and she didn't need this huge, wild horse making any false moves. Spotlight stopped outside of her reach, but he'd come.

She extended her hand and waited. The horse's nostrils quivered and flared, and he took another couple of steps forward.

"How in the world did you do that?" Dwayne whispered.

Satisfaction, combined with relief, filled her, but she refused to smile at the horse. The trainer didn't smile until the horse had a rider on its back.

"Come on, Spotlight," she said again, happiness parading through her when the massive horse took another step and then tapped his nose against her palm.

She dropped her hand to her side and glanced at Dwayne. "All right. Your turn."

CHAPTER EIGHT

Felicity almost laughed at the disbelief on Dwayne's face. He scoffed, the sharp sound sending Spotlight shuffling to the right.

"I can't do that," he said.

"Sure you can," she said. "Use Payday's name. Ask him to come. Wait for him. Show him your hand."

Dwayne looked more uncomfortable than a cowboy should ever be around horses. Felicity wanted to give him the confidence he needed to get Payday to come over from the shady spot next to the barn.

"You're in charge of the horse," she said. "Just like you're in charge of your cowboys. This ranch. Take that same authority, and transfer it to the horse."

He cleared his throat, and she placed her hand on his arm. "No nerves, Dwayne. You're in charge here. They can't think or feel for even a moment that you're not."

Dwayne's body turned toward hers, and he inched closer. "Maybe I need a lesson not in the pasture with the horses."

"You're doin' fine," she said, drawing out the word *fine* the way she'd heard him do before.

"I have no idea what I'm doing," he said darkly, his bass voice rumbling through her chest he stood so close.

"You're asking the horse to come to you," she said. "How would you ask Gaston to do that?"

"I'd say, "Come on, Gaston. Let's go.""

"Same thing here."

Dwayne gave her a dubious look, put some space between them, and lifted his right hand toward the group of horses still hovering near the barn.

"Come on, Payday," he said, his voice clear and loud and authoritative. Felicity tucked her hands in her pockets as she waited for the horse to respond. A sense of peace infused her, something she hadn't felt on her family's ranch in months.

She held onto this feeling, trying to pinpoint what had caused it so she could replicate it in the future.

DWAYNE FELT FOOLISH STANDING THERE WITH HIS EMPTY HAND out, expecting a horse who barely knew his name to come forward. "I haven't had Payday for long," he said.

"Call him again," Felicity said, her voice calm yet absolutely in control.

"Come on, Payday," Dwayne said again. To his surprise the Rocky Mountain chocolate horse turned his head toward him. "Come on."

Payday took his sweet time, but he left the shade and plodded toward Dwayne. "Do I give him a treat?" he asked, suddenly panicking. "Did you bring any hay cubes?"

"He doesn't get a treat for walking over to you. He has to do that every time he's asked. Don't drop your hand." Hers shot out and lifted his. "Focus on him. He has to touch you before we move on."

The Rocky Mountain horse stopped only halfway to him, and

his confidence took a nosedive. "Now what?" he asked out of the side of his mouth.

Felicity stepped over to Spotlight and scrubbed his cheeks, leaving Dwayne with the sight of her buddying up to a wild horse. Leaving him standing there with his hand out.

"Come on, Payday," he said again, a twinge of desperation in his voice, which earned him a sharp look from Felicity. But Payday took a few more steps. Dwayne stared at the horse, beginning a silent battle of wills with the animal. He couldn't lose. Not on top of already being thrown and nearly gored in front of Felicity.

Come on, he prayed silently, refusing to even blink. The horse didn't seem to need to blink either, and Dwayne's eyes started to water.

"Payday," he said, practically begging the horse to just take a few more steps and touch his palm. Maybe tomorrow he would conceal a hay cube in his pocket. "Come on."

By some miracle, the horse plodded forward a few steps and nudged his hand. Joy burst through him, and he couldn't help the smile that exploded onto his face.

"Good," Felicity said. "Now we walk." She edged away from the horse and headed for the fence line. Dwayne hastened to join her, hoping to hold her hand again. He was still sort of shocked she'd let him earlier, right there in the open pasture where anyone could see. He was definitely stunned he'd done it.

They walked along the fence, and Dwayne stepped close but didn't reach for her hand again. Every so often, Felicity would glance behind her and say, "Come on, Spotlight." The horse came with her, with Payday trailing him.

"So," he said, hoping he wasn't about to ruin any chance he might have with Felicity. "You don't have to tell me if you don't want to, but I sense you have a story about your dad."

She sucked in a breath and lifted one hand to rub her opposite arm. He watched the shutters fly over her eyes, and he wanted to block them before they closed completely.

"No judgment here, Felicity." He glanced over his shoulder and added, "Come on, Payday."

They walked the length of one side of the pasture before Felicity said, "My father passed away nine months ago."

Dwayne's heart full-on stopped. His feet stuttered against the ground. His hand started trembling harder. "I'm so sorry, Felicity," he said, pouring every ounce of sympathy he could muster into his tone. "I—I didn't know. I'm sorry."

She flashed him a wounded smile. "It's okay. I—maybe I need to talk about it."

He remained silent so she could say what she wanted, but she just kept walking. The relentless sun beat down on them, and his stomach growled. "You want to come to my house for lunch?" he asked.

She nodded a few times. "Yeah, sure." She turned back to the horses. "We're gonna go for a while, guys. We'll be back soon."

Dwayne stopped walking and twisted around too, only to find all four horses following them in a single-file line along the fence. He marveled at the strength and the soul of Felicity and gazed at her with awe streaming through him.

Her sadness seemed to evaporate like dew under the morning sun, and he reached for her hand again before they started toward his house.

"I JUST CAN'T BELIEVE THAT HORSE." FELICITY CLIPPED THE words out in perfect punctuation to the sound of her boots going up his steps. She rubbed her shoulder as Dwayne followed and opened his front door.

He'd gotten used to their daily routine of training horses in the morning, sharing lunch together at his house, and working around the ranch in the afternoon. She hadn't questioned her role to work around the ranch instead of just training the horses.

"They can't take much more than we're doing in the morning," she'd explained to him when he'd wondered if she had time to be fixing fence posts.

Felicity huffed as she stepped past him and lifted her cowgirl hat from her head. "That Spotlight is so stubborn." She slapped her gloves on the coffee table and went into the kitchen without waiting for Dwayne.

He chuckled. "I had no idea you could get frustrated." He followed her but stopped and leaned against the end of the counter.

She gave him a sour look and pulled open his fridge. "Did you eat all those potatoes?"

Affection pulled through him, and he laughed again. "There's still some in there."

She retrieved the plastic container and put it on the counter. "You saw him try to kick me, right?"

"I saw 'im." Dwayne folded his arms and kept his distance. If he didn't, he couldn't predict what he'd do, because the desire to kiss her tore through him with the force and speed of a tornado.

"I've never had a horse do that before." She put her palms on the counter, leaned into them, and stared at the wall as if it contained the secret for how to train Spotlight.

Dwayne had managed to get a rope around Payday's neck, but Spotlight had steadfastly refused to be touched by more than Felicity's fingertips.

"Did you want some of those meatballs too?" he asked, stepping to her side and popping the lid on the cheesy potatoes his sister had brought him on Tuesday night. There was just enough for one more lunch, and he stuck the container in the microwave and started it.

Felicity didn't answer, and Dwayne let her have a few seconds to herself. Her frustration really was cute to him; he couldn't help it. Had she really never had a horse who didn't bend to her absolute will?

The microwave beeped, signaling that the potatoes were hot,

and Felicity still hadn't moved. Dwayne pulled the food out and dished her some, saying, "So I wanted to ask you a question."

She turned toward him slowly, her eyes taking a few extra moments to focus. When she found him sitting at the small dining room table, she hastened to join him. "I just can't quite figure out what to do next," she said, picking up her fork and staring out the window.

"You've really never had a horse that balks at the rope?"

"Of course I have." She stabbed her fork into her food. "But not for three days in a row, no matter what I try. Not one who tries to kick me when I so much as approach with a rope in my hand."

"He's spirited, all right." Dwayne bit back his question, sure another time would present itself. Hopefully.

"Spirited?" She scoffed and stuck a bite of potatoes in her mouth. After chewing and swallowing, she said, "That horse is a menace."

Dwayne couldn't help it; he tipped his head back and laughed. Only a heartbeat passed before Felicity chortled too. She cut off the sound quickly, and said, "Stop it."

When he didn't, she giggled again.

"Seriously, stop laughing at me."

Dwayne quieted but he couldn't stop smiling. "I'm not laughing at you, sweetheart. You were laughing too." His heart tripped when his ears caught what had come out of his mouth.

Sweetheart.

Her shoulders lifted as she took in a big breath. She'd heard the endearment too, and Dwayne didn't know how to call it back.

"So." He cleared his throat. "I wanted to ask you if you went to church. I thought maybe, if you did, if you'd found one that you like yet, bein' new in town and all, and if you haven't, if you'd like to go with me on Sunday."

Dwayne's lungs felt stuck together as he'd used all his available air to get out the long stream of words. But somehow, he couldn't draw a full breath while he waited for her to answer.

She pushed her potatoes around in her bowl, her focus

completely on them. She hadn't told him much more about her father's death, only that it had been sudden and heartbreaking. They'd spoken of their siblings, and she'd talked a little about her family's ranch. He'd told her about how his parents had met, and why they'd come to Grape Seed Falls.

He'd held her hand in the pasture, on the path back to his house, and on his couch.

"What's the pastor's name?" she finally asked.

"Charlie Gifford."

"Is he old or young?"

Dwayne blinked, wondering what that had to do with her desire to attend church. "He's a few years older than me." He took a bite of his lunch, his mind whirring as he ate. "He has a good way about him. Always speaks about the Savior. I like him."

Truth was, Dwayne was tired of sitting against the wall by himself. So he usually sat with several of the cowboys. Or maybe his parents. They were fine company, but Dwayne didn't want fine. Not anymore.

Now that he'd met Felicity, he knew he could have more than fine. It felt just within his reach, but he couldn't quite grasp it.

Felicity looked up and swept her fingers across the loose hair by her ear. She twisted the lock there and considered him. Dwayne wanted to look away, but he couldn't make himself do it. He watched her soften, watched a playful smile adorn her mouth.

"What time does it start?" she asked.

"Eleven," he forced out through a narrow throat. "I can come pick you up."

She dipped her chin, a beautiful blush blooming in her cheeks. "All right."

"All right." A smile spread his lips.

"Just to warn you, I haven't been to church in a while."

He heard something hidden between the syllables of her words, but he didn't know what. "Why not?" he asked, scooping up another bite of potato.

"I don't know," she said, and Dwayne nodded.

"Fair enough." He hoped she'd figure it out and confide in him. Hoped he could hold her hand during the service. Hoped she would want to find where she fit, because he really hoped to give her space in his heart, on his ranch, in his life.

CHAPTER NINE

Dwayne went to the pasture on Saturday morning, a rope in his hand just like he had the previous day. Payday came over to him without Dwayne having to speak a word. The horse nosed his palm, and Dwayne said, "Good morning to you too." He smiled and kept the coiled rope at his side. "Jinx is comin' in with me. Back up."

He pushed open the gate and gestured for the dog to go in. The border collie seemed bored, but he loved to be with Dwayne. He walked nearly at his heels as Dwayne started along the length of the fence. "C'mon, Payday."

The sky was a light shade of blue this early in the morning, and Dwayne took in a lungful of fresh air. His parents had returned from their fishing trip last night, and his mother hadn't wasted any time insisting that he come to the homestead for breakfast. His sister was coming too, and Dwayne had texted her to ask her to grab him from the pasture when she arrived at the ranch.

He dragged the rope along the rungs, creating an annoying, scratching sound of fiber against wood. Payday didn't startle or dance away. He'd settled a lot in just the few days Dwayne had been working with him.

Probably because you're here every day, he thought. He'd never spent hours every morning training a horse. He didn't have that kind of time. But his cowboys had risen to the task of keeping everything else on the ranch running.

After the first circuit, Dwayne looped the rope and tossed it over Payday's head. The horse closed his eyes almost lazily, and Dwayne led him around again, talking about the things he needed to complete on the ranch that day.

"And then I'm gonna take the ATV out to the north fields," he said. "There's the best grass there, next to the river. Once you're all broken in, I'll take you up there. You're going to love it."

"Talking to your horses again?"

Dwayne spun at the female voice, a half-dozen emotions spiraling through him as he thought, *What's Felicity doing here?*

But it wasn't Felicity. His sister stood there, grinning at him.

"Heather," he said. "You scared me."

She laughed, climbed the fence, and dropped to the ground beside him. "What's this one's name?" She took the rope from him and looked up at the chocolatey brown horse.

Dwayne told her and promptly got her talking about something besides him. "What are you doin' this summer?" he asked.

"Oh, you know."

He didn't, but he said, "Sunbathing, I bet. Or getting your nails done. And reading. You probably read a book every single day."

She laughed again and tossed her sun-kissed brown hair over her shoulder. "All of the above." She sighed happily. "I love summer."

Dwayne much preferred ranching in the cooler months, but summer definitely held some of its magic in the very air. He enjoyed the festivals, and the holidays, and by the end of September, the promise of chili cook-offs and cooler weather.

"So," she said. "I heard a rumor about you."

"Oh boy," he said, squinting into the horizon like there was something important there for him to see. "Who'd you hear it from?"

"Levi Rhodes."

"Levi?" Dwayne repeated. "I can't imagine what he would've told you."

"Said you've been holdin' hands with a pretty brunette." Heather danced in front of Dwayne, bringing Payday up beside him. She looked absolutely gleeful. "True or false?"

Heat filled Dwayne's whole body. "True. But—" He held up his hand before Heather could laugh or shriek or whatever it was she had planned. "How does Levi know that?" He narrowed his eyes at her now. "And when did you talk to him?"

"Oh, I go out to his stables and ride one of his horses every week. He does open riding on Fridays."

Dwayne frowned, trying to make things align in his head. "You can come ride a horse here any time you want."

"Yeah, of course." Heather ducked her hand and fell back into step beside him. Dwayne couldn't help feeling like he was missing an important piece of the puzzle.

"So you talked to him yesterday. I haven't seen him in days. He doesn't come out here."

"No, but Gabe was there helping yesterday, and he brought it up. Levi asked about Farrah? What's her name?"

"Felicity."

"Yeah, Felicity. Levi wanted to know if she was any good, and Gabe was telling him all about it."

"And you were...eavesdropping?"

"Saddling." She scoffed and lightly punched his bicep. "I was nearby, saddling my horse. Can I help it if Gabe has a loud voice? No, I cannot." She grinned at him. "So you're holding Felicity's hand, huh? Over your female fast?"

He rolled his eyes. "I was never on a female fast."

"Dwayne, you haven't dated since Serenity broke your heart."

"Well, it takes a while to get all the pieces glued back together." He didn't want to think about Serenity. "Besides, I don't see you datin' anyone. Not since Teddy."

"Oh, Teddy." She waved her hand like the man had meant

nothing to her. But she'd spent an hour talking about him at Thanksgiving two years ago. An *hour*. Talking about one person. She'd clearly been smitten with him, and they'd dated for almost a year before he just up and left town one day. Heather hadn't come out to the ranch for three months after Teddy's departure, and Dwayne never had figured out why.

"So, are you dating again?" he asked.

"Nope." She made a popping sound on the P and giggled. "Grape Seed Falls needs some new bachelors to move into town."

Before he'd met Felicity, Dwayne would've added, "And some bachelorettes." Now, he simply smiled and said, "You'll find someone, Heather."

"Really?" A bit of incredulity crept into her voice. "Where do you think I'll meet them? On the playground while I'm doing recess duty? Or wait. At the Laundromat while I'm there on Saturday evening because my machine is on the fritz. *Again*."

"I can come look at it."

"Dad's already coming after breakfast." She tucked her arm in his. "And you know, no one who's at the Laundromat on the weekend is worth meeting."

He detected her sadness, and maybe some loneliness. Dwayne knew, because he'd drowned in loneliness for a solid six months after Serenity had broken up with him. "Come on, Heather. Give yourself some credit."

"You're right," she said. "I'm not going to do my laundry until Monday."

He laughed along with her, unlooped the rope from Payday's neck, and gave the horse a pat. "See you tomorrow," he whispered before following his sister and his dog over to the homestead.

He'd barely opened the kitchen door when his mother appeared. "You're dating Felicity Lightburne?"

"What?" He glanced over her head to see Heather wearing a half-gleeful, half-horrified expression.

"I didn't know it was a secret," she said.

"Isn't she our new horse trainer?" His father stepped to his mother's side.

Dwayne groaned, wishing he could turn around and go to his house. Cold cereal would be better than the third degree from his parents.

SUNDAY MORNING, FELICITY SPENT THE HALF HOUR BEFORE THE sun rose walking the streets of Grape Seed Falls. Her stomach wasn't happy with her, though she hadn't eaten much for dinner the night before.

No, she had nerves assaulting her, making her sick, tormenting her.

Maybe just call Dwayne and say you can't go to church, she thought. Then she amended it to, *Don't call. He'll be able to read the anxiety in your voice. Text him. Text him and tell him you can't do it.*

She entered her bungalow and her eyes landed on the dress she'd spent most of yesterday afternoon shopping for. She hadn't brought any skirts or dresses from home, as she hadn't planned on attending church or anything else that required her to dress up.

The fabric of the dress was light and airy, almost like silk. The maxi dress was cream-colored, with bright blue, red, and green flowers decorating it. It skimmed the floor, but with the right shoes, she felt like a princess wearing it.

She wondered what Dwayne would think. Would he even recognize her without the cowgirl hat, the jeans, the boots?

With hours to go before she needed to be ready, she set a pot of coffee to brew and she headed down the hall to the spare bedroom. She'd set up a folding table, which she'd pushed against the wall with the large window that overlooked the backyard.

Whiskers jumped up onto the table at the same time Felicity sat down at it. She pulled the hatband she'd started on Friday night toward her and started threading on the next bead in the pattern. She loved working with her hands, and this delicate work with jewels, beads, and fibers was just as rewarding as the more physical labor of training horses.

The cat curled into a ball and purred, making Felicity realize how simple her life had become. She didn't need music to entertain her. Or a schedule filled with dozens of activities. She'd never lived away from home before, and she marveled at that fact now because of how much she loved this sense of independence she'd found.

"This one's almost done," she told Whiskers. "Should I make you a collar next?" She needed to craft something besides hatbands, because she had at least a dozen. No, what she really needed was someone to give the hatbands too. A friend. A sister-in-law. A charitable group. Something.

Out of the list, Felicity thought she could definitely use a friend the most, and she abandoned her crafting with a wild idea in her mind. She was decent with a recipe, and it didn't take long to put together a batch of chocolate chip cookies.

She'd seen people coming and going on the street where she lived, and she wondered if maybe the friend she needed was right next door. Or across the street. Or down on the corner.

And there was only one way to find out.

An hour later, armed with a plate of cookies, Felicity went down her front steps and across the lawn. She paused on the sidewalk, glancing left and right and facing forward again. She had three options.

Which way should I go? she prayed, sure the Lord didn't care who she gave cookies to on a Sunday morning.

She heard nothing, felt nothing. As usual, God didn't concern Himself with her and her relentless begging. But she couldn't stand on the sidewalk like a statue forever. She turned to her right and went to the cottage next door.

A woman answered it only a few seconds after Felicity knocked. "Hello," she said brightly. "I moved in next door last week. I'm Felicity Lightburne."

The woman's smile was instant, and she accepted the cookies

with a grateful, "Thank you. My son has been sick, and well, there's nothing worse than a cold in the summer." She leaned in the doorway, wearing her capri sweatpants and an orange tank top. Her blonde hair was piled into a messy bun on top of her head, and she seemed gracious and generous and very Texan to Felicity. "I've been fixin' to make him breakfast, but well, I haven't done it yet." She laughed a little, and Felicity liked her.

"I hope he likes the cookies," Felicity said, unsure of what to do next. She'd had friends in high school, of course. Friends around town in Marysville. But she didn't spend weekends or evenings with her girlfriends. She'd spent them with her family, or her horses, or by herself.

And oh, how she was tired of being by herself.

"You want to come in and meet him?" she asked.

"Oh, if he's sick, I'll just be in the way."

"It's fine." The woman turned and called over her shoulder, "Jonah, come meet our neighbor." She looked back at Felicity. "I'm Capri Calhoun." She beamed down at a little boy who was probably eight or nine. "This is my son, Jonah."

Felicity smiled at them both. "Nice to meet you. Have you lived in Grape Seed Falls long?"

"Just since Dad died," Jonah said.

Felicity sucked in a breath and her eyes flew to Capri's. A twinge of hurt passed across the other woman's expression, but she wiped it away quickly. "Motorcycle accident, almost six years ago," she explained. "We've lived right here in this house ever since." She kneaded her son closer, her hand strong and tight on his shoulder.

"I'm so sorry," Felicity said, the grief from her father's death flowing freely now. She usually kept it so boxed up, held it so tight, but she couldn't seem to get a grip on it at all. The pain in Capri's eyes...and it had been *six years* since her husband's death.

Would Felicity have to suffer for that long with this crippling sadness?

She shook her head as if that alone could rid her of her thoughts. "Well, it was nice to meet you Carpi. Jonah." She smiled again, but it felt wobbly around the edges. "I should go get ready for church." She started down the steps.

"Where y'all goin'?" Capri called.

Felicity turned back to her. "I'm not really sure. My...boss is coming to pick me up, me being new in town and all." She'd almost used another B-word for Dwayne, but holding his hand and eating lunch together didn't make him her boyfriend. She wasn't sure what would, as she hadn't really ever had a man she'd label as her boyfriend.

"I hope it's the one on Elberta Street," Capri said. "That's the best one."

"I guess we'll see." Her voice shook a little, and she wasn't even sure why. Probably because her mind couldn't get past Dwayne becoming her boyfriend.

Dwayne. Boyfriend.

Boyfriend. Dwayne.

Her heart started galloping in her chest, and she practically sprinted back to the safety of her bungalow. She pressed her back into the closed door, trying to catch her breath. She let her eyes drift shut, and she imagined what it would be like to kiss the tall, handsome cowboy. Would his hand tremble as he held her face in his palm? What would he taste like? How would she stay standing, seeing as her knees had just gone weak with the very thought of kissing him?

Felicity exhaled slowly, deliberately pushing out her breath. *First things first*, she told herself, and that included seeing how Dwayne would react to her when she was all made up, looking like a Southern belle and not a country cowgirl.

CHAPTER TEN

F elicity cried out when knocking sounded on her front door. And she'd been ready and waiting for the past fifteen minutes. She strode on sandaled feet to the door and opened it.

The simple sight of Dwayne stole her breath. She stared at his clean-shaven face, his charcoal-colored cowboy hat—clearly one that didn't get worn every day around the ranch—and his tall, trim body decked out in a white shirt, a blue paisley tie, and dark gray slacks.

He gazed right back at her, the electricity popping and zipping between them as if someone had thrown a switch.

"You're—" His voice came out strangled and hoarse, and he cleared his throat. "What a pretty dress."

"I like your hat," she said, playing along to a game where she didn't know the rules.

He offered her his elbow. "Should we go?"

She slipped her hand over his bare forearm, a thrill riding all the way down to her toes and back.

"Somethin' in your house smells good," he said as she joined him on the porch and pulled the door closed behind her.

"I made chocolate chip cookies this morning."

"Is that so?" He gave her sideways look as the walked down her sidewalk toward the truck.

"We can come back here after church and eat them," she said. "I mean, if you want."

He opened the passenger-side door of his truck but didn't move out of the way so she could get in. "I was hopin' to take you to lunch over in Cleargrass," he said. "There's a really great barbeque place there that does brisket and pork ribs on Sundays."

"Brisket and pork ribs?"

"Don't tell me you don't like barbeque." He gazed at her evenly, and she sensed her answer would mean a great deal to him.

"Who doesn't like barbeque?" she asked.

"There are some people." He didn't so much as blink.

Felicity felt the words damming up behind her tongue. She couldn't quite order them, but when she opened her mouth, she said, "My father made the best smoked brisket in the whole state."

Dwayne's eyebrows went up. "Is that right?" He reached up and trailed the back of his hand down the side of her face. "Your father...you miss him?"

"Very much." Felicity felt like she'd cut herself open and letting him in. It hurt, but it felt good too. "He...was my best friend."

Dwayne cocked his head and studied her. "Really? That's interesting. Usually daughters are best friends with their mothers."

Felicity considered him, considered how much to tell him. If she wanted him to be her boyfriend, wanted to kiss him, she'd need to share things with him. "My mother was, well, let's just say she was disappointed that I was more cowgirl than girl."

He scanned her from her nearly bare feet to the waves she'd put in her hair. "She obviously hasn't seen you on your way to church." He leaned forward, and Felicity froze as if someone had poured liquid nitrogen into her bloodstream. She inhaled, taking in the masculine scent of his skin, the minty quality of his breath.

Her eyes drifted closed as if she'd receive his kiss, but his mouth moved past hers. His hands encircled her waist and he embraced her, his face in the hollow of her neck. She felt strong and weak at the same time. Happy and sad. Beautiful and tired.

"Let's skip church," he said, his voice husky and sending tremors through her torso.

"All right," she whispered. "Want to go to Cleargrass right now?"

"Yeah." He pulled back and finally stepped to the side so she could climb into the cab. He helped her up, closed the door and rounded the front of the truck while Felicity tried to sort through the tangled mess of emotions in the back of her throat.

DWAYNE WASN'T ONE TO SKIP CHURCH JUST BECAUSE. BUT something told him that Felicity didn't need a sermon today. She just needed to be...free. Needed someone to talk to. Needed somewhere to just be herself.

He didn't think she could look any better than she did in a pair of jeans, but the floral dress had definitely got his pulse pounding. She curved and swelled in all the right places, and Dwayne couldn't help reaching for her.

She slid over on the bench seat and twined her fingers with his. After they'd left the town of Grape Seed Falls behind, she laid her head against his shoulder, and the tension he'd sensed from her disappeared completely.

He hummed along to the song on the radio, content to be with her even in the silence. He hadn't felt this way about anyone in so long, he wasn't sure if he could trust the tranquil feelings or not.

"You have a beautiful voice," she said, interrupting him in the middle of a chorus. He hadn't even realized he'd started singing.

Dwayne squeezed her fingers and ten minutes later, they pulled up to the restaurant. The term "restaurant" was generous, but there was already a line, and it was barely lunchtime yet.

"Honey's Hickory," Felicity read once he'd helped her out of the truck. She gazed up at the sign that had weathered five decades of brutal Texas sun, wind, and probably the occasional hailstorm. Her eyes met his, and he saw a hint of trepidation in her dark depths.

"It's good," he said. "C'mon."

They joined the line, and the silence didn't feel so comfortable anymore. "My sister is gonna call any second," he said.

Felicity's eyebrows went up. "How do you know?"

"Because church started a few minutes ago, and I'm not there. Just wait and see."

"Does she keep tabs on you all the time?"

His phone rang, and he pulled it from his pocket and turned it toward Felicity. "See?" He swiped the call to voicemail. "And no, she doesn't keep tabs on me. But I told her I was bringing you to church, so when we don't show up...." He shrugged. "She's not usually too nosy. I think you'd like her."

Felicity hadn't properly met any of his family yet. A quick nod before ducking out of his hospital room didn't count. His parents had been gone all week, and Heather didn't make it a habit to come out to the ranch during the week all that often.

"This might surprise you, but I don't have a lot of girlfriends."

Dwayne tucked her hand into his. "As long as you don't have a lot of boyfriends either."

She laughed and nudged him with her shoulder. Sobering, she said, "Not a lot of those, no."

"No?" He tugged her closer, and she came. "Not interested in a boyfriend?"

She glanced up at him and got stuck in the moment with him. He couldn't look away, and everything surrounding him faded into nothing. There was only Felicity, and the tender, vulnerable vibe streaming from her eyes.

Dwayne's brain felt like it had during the years he was recuperating from his traumatic brain injury. Slow, and sluggish, and stale. His body seemed to know what to do though, because his free hand settled on her hip, and his back bent down to get his mouth closer to hers.

Someone spoke, but Dwayne couldn't make sense of it. His nerves fired every nanosecond, and the only thing moving was his feet so he could get closer to Felicity.

"Dwayne," she said, but it wasn't in the low, sexy voice he'd expected right before he kissed her.

He became aware of her grip on his hand pulling him forward at the same time a man said, "What are you? Brain dead? The line is way up there."

Dwayne came back to reality, and he only had time to swing his head toward the man before Felicity stepped past him. "It's ten feet. Back off."

"Look, you guys need to stop—" He stopped when she held up her hand, and Dwayne would've too. The anger streaming from her sent a shockwave through him.

"*You* need to stop," she said in a freaky, calm voice. "We're moving. And no one is brain dead." She glared at him for another three heartbeats, and then she spun and stalked past Dwayne, closing the distance between them and the line that had moved forward.

"Can you believe that guy?" she asked when Dwayne joined her, certainly loud enough for the man to hear.

"It's fine," Dwayne muttered. He tucked his hands in his pockets, foolishness racing through him. Had he seriously almost kissed her in a barbeque line? With dozens of people watching?

Humiliation joined the tantrum happening in his chest. He was aware that sometimes he needed extra processing time. Sometimes he required extra periods of rest. But it had been almost eight years since his injury, and he functioned pretty well most of the time.

"It's not fine," she said. "No one should go around calling someone else brain dead." She shot a dirty look behind her, completely unafraid of the man there. "Have you ever met someone who was brain dead?" She cocked her hip and folded her arms. "They don't eat barbeque, I can tell you that." Her chest heaved, and Dwayne realized her reaction wasn't about him at all.

He watched her, watched the storm as it marched across her face, watched as the anger and the bravado faded, leaving only sadness and tears.

He didn't need extra processing time to know what to do. Dwayne stepped closer to her and drew her into his chest.

CHAPTER ELEVEN

"Hey, it's okay," he said, stroking her hair while her tears stained his white shirt right over his heart. Her arms came around him, and she held onto him tight, like she might not be able to hold herself up without his assistance.

He caught the eye of the man behind them, and the other guy looked ashamed and uncomfortable. Dwayne wasn't sure why Felicity had acted the way she had and then broken down. It didn't really matter. She stood in his arms, and she belonged there.

He inched her forward when the line moved. "You know, for a minute there, I thought you were defending me."

She sniffed and pulled away enough to look up into his face. "You?"

He hadn't planned on detailing his injuries while in line for brisket, but he figured now was as good a time as any. "Yeah, my arm and hand shake from permanent nerve damage because of a traumatic brain injury I sustained in the Marines." He marveled at how smooth his voice said the words. How calm his pulse beat in his chest. He normally felt a lot more embarrassment when talking about his time overseas and how it had ended.

She blinked, her tears sticking to her eyelashes and making her beautiful and vulnerable. She slipped her hands along his sides and stepped away from him, glancing around at the crowd outside the restaurant.

"I didn't know you were in the Marines."

"Yeah, I told you when we were waiting for the ambulance."

Felicity cocked her head like she was searching her memories. "I guess you did. And Atlas, he was your dog."

"Military combat dog," he said. "Trained with—"

"Explosives," they said at the same time.

Felicity wiped her face and gave him a shaky smile. "I remember. You didn't mention getting hurt." Her eyes screamed her curiosity, her desire to know the whole story.

"No, I didn't." Dwayne gazed past her into the brilliant sunshine and Texas landscape that ran for miles. "Atlas was the best at finding buried IEDs. One day, we'd been out for hours, and he'd found one every few feet." He stepped forward when the line moved. Only a few people remained between them and the order counter. Maybe he could get this story out and over with by then.

"We came under fire, and we had to take shelter off the road. Well, we didn't have time for Atlas to locate the buried bombs, and we triggered one. We were both injured."

He'd come home after that injury—his first and only incident in Iraq. While he wasn't glad he'd experienced the explosion, things had turned out okay. Atlas had been on his last mission anyway, and Dwayne was able to adopt him after the military retired him from service. They'd lived a good life on the ranch since, even if Atlas couldn't participate in driving the herd from one place to another because of his anxiety, and Dwayne's fingers shook.

Felicity stepped closer to him. "You were brain dead?" Her voice came out hushed, reverent almost.

"I was in a coma for eight days," Dwayne said. "I have a traumatic brain injury. It took me three years before I finally felt like I was thinking clearly again." He lifted his hand, which shook from the elbow down. Tremors he used to hate, to hide, but that he was beginning to...something. He didn't hate them anymore, he supposed.

"This is the biggest evidence of the injury now."

"How long ago did this happen?" she asked.

"Eight years." The line moved forward again, and Dwayne fell silent, relieved that story was out between them. He hadn't had to share it with anyone in a long time, and giving some of the burden to Felicity felt cleansing. Freeing. Bonding.

FELICITY FELT AS THOUGH SHE'D BOARDED A ROLLER COASTER when she'd gotten in line for a simple plate of barbeque. First from the highs of being so close to Dwayne. They'd almost kissed, right there in line. Then to hearing the words "brain dead."

Her anger had been swift and consuming. She hadn't meant to be snappy and rude to a stranger, but really, it was a matter of a few feet.

She was still surprised she'd cried. She hadn't cried over her father's death since the day of his funeral last October. She'd vowed she wouldn't live under that cloud the way her mother had. She'd survived the holidays by taking Linus and Lucy out to a cabin on her family's property and avoiding everyone. That was when she knew she needed to find somewhere else to work.

She'd talked with her brother, Gordon, and together, they'd planned her departure from the ranch. Parker, her youngest brother, had discovered her plan and supported her too. Her mother...well, her mother was still coming to terms with a lot of things. Felicity leaving home was only one of them.

"We're next. So you want brisket and ribs?" Dwayne asked, bringing her back to this moment in time.

Felicity nodded as she took a deep breath. "And cole slaw, and baked beans, and some of that potato salad." She beamed up at Dwayne, who chuckled and shook his head. He probably felt like he was on a roller coaster too, and Felicity's self-consciousness kicked in.

She appreciated that Dwayne had shared his past with her, and she wanted to do the same. "So," she said, and he looked at her. "My father had a stroke and fell. He didn't wake up from his coma and lost all brain activity." She hugged herself as if cold, though the sun was near its pinnacle. "He was brain dead, and we took him off life support."

Felicity glanced behind her to find the man who'd started all of this wearing a horrified look.

"I'm so sorry," he said. "I didn't—I wouldn't—"

"It's okay," she said at the same time Dwayne's fingers closed over hers. "How could you know?"

"Next," the cashier called, and Dwayne tugged her to the order window. He listed all the things they wanted, and then turned to the man behind him. "We'll get yours too." He stepped to the side to make room. "Tell 'im what you want."

"No." The man shook his head. "I'll get theirs." He moved into position and put in his order, paid, and moved out of line. "My name's Collin. I'm really sorry."

"Don't worry about it," Felicity said as she took a plate laden with brisket and baked beans from a server. "From the looks of this, I'd yell at the people in front of me to get going too."

The scent of the tomato-based sauce, the tang of the vinegar, and the heat through the paper plate set her mouth watering.

"You've never been to Honey's?" Collin asked.

"This would be the first time." Felicity watched Dwayne collect forks and napkins. "My...friend said it's the best barbeque in Hill Country."

Collin collected his order too. "Well, he's right." He tipped his cowboy hat and moved away, clearly not wanting to join them for lunch.

"There's shade over there." Dwayne nodded with the brim of his hat to her left. She went in that direction, everything inside her settling down. Dwayne hadn't had time to react to how her father had passed, and Felicity didn't think the conversation was over. But at least she'd trusted him enough to tell him.

She'd never done that before.

And she'd never had such juicy and delicious brisket either. She moaned on the first bite, not even caring if she had sauce all over her face.

Dwayne sat across from her on the end of the picnic table and stared at her for an extra beat, his blue eyes darkening with desire before he chuckled. "I'm glad you like it."

"We should come here every weekend," she said, reaching for a napkin.

"I'll cater it for our next ranch event," he said. "Maybe my parents would like to have a Fourth of July picnic at Grape Seed." He seemed serious, and Felicity just smiled.

"I'm real sorry about your dad," he said, leaning forward. "Making a decision like that...." He shook his head and hadn't taken a single bite of his food yet. "My mom—" He cleared his throat. "My mom said for a few hours while I was in the coma, one of the doctors thought my brain activity had ceased. She said she couldn't even imagine taking me off life support."

Felicity didn't know what to say. Her heart bounced around in her chest, beating irregularly as if it had forgotten how to do its basic function. She forked a bite of baked beans into her mouth just for something to do.

He stared at his plate, his cowboy hat blocking the view of his face. "She went to the chapel in the hospital and prayed." Dwayne lifted his eyes to Felicity's. "Says that right after that, my brain readings improved."

Felicity could barely swallow her food. She too was well-versed with praying in a hospital chapel. Why hadn't God answered any of her pleas to help her father? Did God love his mother more than he loved Felicity? How could He save Dwayne and not her dad?

She hadn't talked about her faltering faith since her father's death, not even with Gordon. Certainly not with her mother, who'd seemed to make it her personal mission to help everyone around them who was also suffering. As if that would somehow ease her own heartache.

"What's wrong?" Dwayne asked, his voice barely carrying across the picnic table.

Felicity shook her head, willing herself not to cry again.

"I didn't mean to upset you," he said. "I was just saying that I can't imagine having to make a decision like that. It must've been terribly hard." He watched her without a shred of guile in his expression. The man was simply good.

"It was hard." She cleared her throat. "And I don't go to church because God didn't answer my prayers the way he answered your mom's."

CHAPTER TWELVE

Dwayne's fork froze halfway to his mouth with his first bite of food.

Felicity gave a light laugh that didn't mirror how she felt inside. "I had to go buy this dress yesterday," she admitted. "I didn't actually bring any church clothes with me."

He just nodded and said, "That's understandable."

Was it? Felicity wasn't even sure herself, but she was desperate for something lighter to talk about. All the drama, the crying, the confessions, they didn't belong with such delicious food and such handsome company.

"Let's talk about something else for a while," she said.

"I have an obsession with guacamole," he said. "We can talk about that."

Felicity couldn't help the laugh that burst from her mouth. "Food obsessions. Yes, let's go down this path."

"What's one of yours?"

She took another bite of brisket. "Meat, obviously."

"I already told you about my caramel popcorn addiction." He finally took his first bite of coleslaw.

"Chicken pot pie," she said. "I can't get enough of it."

He smiled, revealing his straight, white teeth. She liked making him smile. Wanted to see him do that everyday and be the reason he did.

"Let's see...oh, bacon. Everyone loves bacon."

Felicity gestured to the meat on her plate. "Salted cured pork. What's not to love?"

"I'll tell you what I don't love. Lasagna."

"Really?" She giggled as a breeze tickled her arms. "What don't you like about it?"

"My mom used to make it when I was growing up." He took a big swallow of his iced tea. "She put these huge fennel seeds in the sauce. I *hated* those."

"No fennel seeds. Got it."

"Do you do a lot of cooking?"

"Not a ton," she said. "But my mother managed to make me proficient in the kitchen." Felicity flashed him a smile that felt crumbly around the edges. "She's happy about that, at least."

Dwayne reached over and touched her hand, his fingers there and then gone. His skin on hers gave her courage for some reason. Made her feel worthy of something she hadn't thought herself worthy of in a long time. Love. Acceptance.

"And for the record, I really don't like cantaloupe," she said in an attempt to distract herself from such deep, self-probing thoughts.

"Oh, that's a shame," he said in a playful, flirtatious tone. "There's nothing better than cold melon on a hot summer day."

Felicity smiled at the same time she rolled her eyes. It was nice to have him to talk to, as she hadn't had someone to share her life with in a while. Even before her father's stroke and death, Felicity hadn't really confided in him the things she'd needed to. Her worries over only having horses for friends. Over growing old alone, with only the ranch to show others what her life had meant.

As Dwayne cleared their empty plates and took her hand in his with a quiet, "Want to walk a little?" Felicity realized with crystal clear clarity what she'd been missing in Marysville.

Dwayne Carver.

She stepped with him, the strength of his presence next to her comforting and deep. It seemed natural to send a prayer of gratitude to the Lord for leading her to Grape Seed Falls and the ranch there which needed a horse trainer. So she did.

But really, she wondered if God had known all along that it was Felicity who needed the ranch, needed Dwayne, in her life.

DWAYNE DROVE TOWARD HIS SISTER'S PLACE AFTER DROPPING Felicity back at her house. He'd spent the drive back to Grape Seed Falls in near-panic mode as he contemplated kissing Felicity before separating for the evening.

He hadn't known if he should walk her to her front door or not. Hadn't wanted to kiss her in broad daylight, with the possibility of her neighbors seeing. Didn't think he could walk her to her door and not kiss her.

So he'd sat in his truck and said, "Thanks for comin' with me. I had a real great time. See you tomorrow."

She'd echoed the words back to him, tucked her hair, and scampered up the front walk to her door.

And he'd been driving in circles around town, trying to decide if he wanted more company—especially Heather's—or if he should head back to the ranch and go through everything alone.

In the end, he pulled into Heather's driveway and made his way to her porch. She exited the house before he arrived and leaned against the pillar. "Well, well, well. Look who decided to show up." She grinned and filled the air with a laugh.

"I need some advice." He climbed the steps and went inside. "Do you have any coffee?"

"Coffee? Oh boy." She closed the door behind him, sealing in all the blessed air conditioning, and gestured him into the kitchen. "Gonna be a long night?"

"I'm fixin' to ask for your help," he said. "That requires caffeine."

She swatted him as she passed and turned on the water to fill the coffee pot. "So you go to pick up Felicity for church and then you two disappear. Sounds risqué."

"We went to Honey's Hickory. Nothing risqué about barbeque."

"Our mother was speculating from here to Vegas about what you two were doing."

Dwayne settled onto a barstool at Heather's counter. "Our mother has an overactive imagination."

"She got married when she was nineteen," Heather said. "I think she's actually disappointed in us."

Dwayne chuckled and said, "Nah. She told me lots of times 'Don't get married too soon, Dwayne. Go see the world. Do something before you can't.'"

Heather turned from where she was scooping coffee granules into the filter. "She said that?"

"More than once. I don't think the Marines was what she meant." His parents hadn't exactly been disappointed, but they hadn't been pleased either. After all, they'd already seen the dangers of war with Dwayne's cousin, Squire. He'd joined the Army and been through a lot before he was ultimately injured and honorably discharged too.

"She never told me that," Heather said, returning to her task. "I'm sure I've disappointed her by remaining single for so long." She spoke in a quiet way that alerted Dwayne to her pain.

"You'll find someone, Heather."

She tossed him a glare over her shoulder. "We've already talked about this." She finished prepping the coffee and joined him at the bar. "I want details about you and Felicity."

Dwayne had come here of his own free will, so he heaved a breath and started talking. He finished with, "So yeah. That's it."

"You didn't even walk her to the door?"

"It's four o'clock in the afternoon."

"So you think a kiss can only happen after dark? Is that it?"

"No." A flush rose through his chest. "I'm...what are we if I kiss her? You know? She works at the ranch. What if we break up?"

Heather stirred her second cup of coffee, the first getting drained while Dwayne had related everything that had happened between him and Felicity over the past week. His sister at least seemed to be thinking about his questions.

"Well, since you don't exactly date that much, I think if you kiss Felicity, she'd be your girlfriend."

Dwayne tried to swallow, but his throat was so tight, he couldn't. He'd thought the same. If he kissed someone he felt as strongly about as he did Felicity, she'd definitely be his girlfriend. After all, he didn't go around kissing every woman he met. Or even meeting women.

He wasn't sure how to feel about having a girlfriend after being single for so long. Part of him wanted to have that other person to confide in, to talk to, to have and to hold. Part of him thought he was doing just fine on his own. Sure, maybe the evenings were lonely sometimes, with just him and the dogs and that silent guitar, but at least his heart was whole.

"She does work at the ranch," Heather said. "But I don't see why it matters. You run the ranch, not the horse training."

"I run it all."

"But you don't have to. If you broke up, you could get Kurt to oversee what Felicity does. You wouldn't have to talk to her or anything."

Dwayne couldn't imagine what it would take to make him want to avoid Felicity. Every cell in his body and brain right now wanted to be with her, talk to her, learn more about her, kiss her.

Kiss her.

He really wanted to kiss her.

"I guess that's a good point." His voice came out a bit stran-gled, and he swallowed a mouthful of coffee to clear the emotion. "I—she seems, I don't know. Broken up about her father's death."

"I'm sure she is."

"How do I handle that delicately?"

"Same way you did today. Ask her questions. Let her talk. Hold her when she cries."

Dwayne hadn't thought he'd done anything special. Certainly not anything grand or helpful. But maybe he had. Maybe just being there and offering a shoulder to cry on and a listening ear had been enough.

He finished his coffee and stood. "Thanks, Heather." He hugged his sister, fiercely glad he had her to talk to. "Want me to set you up with one of the cowboys? Every one of 'em out there is single. They're not bad guys."

She cast her eyes toward the ceiling as if praying for patience. "They're *cowboys*, Dwayne."

"You like cowboys."

"I've dated too many of them to like them." She sniffed and Dwayne sensed she was hiding something. What, he didn't know.

"So which one do you want to go out with?" he asked.

Heather met his eye with a wary edge in hers. "Promise you won't laugh?"

Dwayne raised his right hand in the Boy Scout salute. "Scout's honor."

"Well...." Heather shuffled her feet and couldn't look at him. Her face turned a bright shade of red, and Dwayne chuckled.

"Oh, you really like this man."

"He doesn't work at your ranch."

"Oh, even more mysterious."

"But you know him."

"So am I guessing?"

She shrugged and didn't offer a name, so Dwayne started thinking. "I know him. He doesn't work at the ranch. He's a cowboy...." Honestly, it could be anyone who lived in Grape Seed Falls. The town was surrounded by half a dozen ranches, twice that many orchards, and parks and recreational areas that used horses. Even the mailman wore a cowboy hat on his route.

"I don't know, Heather. Just tell me."

"You talked to him this week."

"And he doesn't work at the ranch?" Dwayne had only gone to—"Levi?"

Heather's blush intensified, if that were even possible.

Dwayne's brain clicked through pieces, taking precious seconds to make them fit together. "Is that why you go ride at his place every Friday?"

"He doesn't even know I'm alive," Heather whispered. "It's pathetic, really." She seemed so broken that Dwayne's heart cracked for his sister.

"I'm sure he knows you're alive. I'll talk to him."

"You absolutely will not." Heather looked up with fire in her eyes. "I'm—managing." She choked out the last word.

Dwayne didn't know what to say, so he pulled her into another hug. "I won't say anything. But he's a fool if he doesn't see you standing right in front of him. Someone ought to tell him." Dwayne wasn't sure where Levi was on the girlfriend spectrum. He wasn't dating anyone that Dwayne knew of, but Dwayne didn't keep tabs on who was with whom around town.

"But it's not going to be you." Heather pulled away and flashed one of her brilliant smiles. "Now you better go let Mom and Dad know you didn't get married this afternoon."

That was a conversation Dwayne didn't want to have, but he headed for the door with, "All right. See you later, sis."

He didn't go straight home, though. As the sun sank toward the west horizon, he drove down Bartlett Street one more time, his craving to kiss Felicity warring with his duty to get home and get ready for another long week of ranching.

Please help her, he prayed as her bungalow came into view. *Heal her hurt. Let her know You care about her, even though her dad died when she asked You to save him.*

She hadn't said those words exactly, but he'd understood her meaning all the same. Dwayne hadn't spent any time wondering why he'd had to go through a bombing. Why his life had been spared. Why he'd had to learn to speak and think and sleep through the night again. He'd accepted God's will for his life, but he knew that wasn't an easy thing to do.

"Help me help her," he whispered as he turned at the end of the street and went by the Hammond's peach orchard. "If I can, let me help her."

CHAPTER THIRTEEN

Dwayne's radio went off before he'd even finished dressing in the morning. "Coyotes in the herd in sector nine." The distance and warbling of Kurt's voice didn't erase his concern.

Dwayne grabbed his hat, stuffed his feet into his boots, and left his house. He hadn't eaten breakfast or brushed his teeth. Didn't matter. His cattle were more precious than calories or cavities.

He normally parked his truck in the four-bay shed on the ranch and took the ATV to his house. So he only had that vehicle for transportation. Dwayne swung into the open-air seat and started the engine, his heart thrumming along with the vehicle.

Kurt kept the updates going on the radio, so by the time Dwayne arrived in sector nine, he knew exactly what to expect. Three downed cows that needed veterinary care, and a length of fence that needed to be repaired.

Kurt stood over one of the cows with Austin, and Dwayne was not prepared for the blood, though he should've been. His stomach turned as he climbed from the ATV and saw the clawed flank and bit hind legs on the cow.

"Still alive?" he asked, taking in the absolute stillness of the animal.

"Barely," Kurt said. "Doc just got to the ranch. She's on her way out now."

Dwayne nodded and scrubbed his hand up the back of his neck. "And the coyotes are gone?"

"Shane shot one," he said. "The others scattered."

"And Gabe is bringing out the fencing supplies?"

"Shoulda been right behind you."

Dwayne nodded, clapped Kurt on the back, and headed toward the next cow lying on the ground. The rest of the cattle had moved away and watched from a distance. The purr of a motor met Dwayne's ears just as he reached the cow. Without nearly as much blood, he wasn't as worried about the survival of this animal.

Gabe arrived, and Dwayne helped him unload the chicken wire and staple guns. He got to work on fixing the fence by following Gabe after he cut away the broken wire with a pair of metal cutters. Austin and Dwayne pulled the new section of wire tight, and Kurt stapled it into place.

Ka-chuck, ka-chuck, ka-chuck. The echo of the staple gun tore through the otherwise serene countryside.

Dwayne exhaled and reached for another roll of wire. His arm scraped along the top of it and pain shot through his system. He yanked back and touched the back of his forearm, his fingers coming away sticky with his own blood.

His head swam, and he drew in a long, deep breath of oxygen to center himself. The blue sky blurred with the golden ground, and he reached out to find something to hold onto. There was only empty air.

His empty stomach turned, and he wiped his dirty fingers on his jeans. *It's just a little scrape*, he told himself. He could tolerate the torn up flesh of one of his cows, but not the sight of his own blood.

The ATV. He stumbled in that direction like he'd had too much to drink. Kurt called to him, but Dwayne couldn't locate the location of the sound. In the next moment, a hand landed on his elbow, steadying him.

"You're bleeding," Kurt said.

Dwayne kept moving toward the ATV, collapsing into the driver's seat when he arrived. "Just a scrape," he said. "On the chicken wire."

Kurt wouldn't relinquish his arm, and he peered at the wound. "This is more than a scrape, boss."

Dwayne didn't look at it, but tried to get his vision to focus, the horizon to still, his head to re-attach to his body. After thirty seconds, he started to feel more normal—just in time for the vet to arrive.

Another cowboy, Sawyer, helped carry her bags toward the most injured cow, and Dwayne got up to do what the owner of a ranch did—make decisions and pay bills and be responsible for everything.

"He's bleeding," Kurt said, never more than a foot from Dwayne.

"I'm fine," he said. "Hey, Lis."

Alyssa Turner, the veterinarian who always came out to Grape Seed greeted him and then glanced at his arm. "Let me wrap it, and that should keep it until you can get back to your house." She pulled out a roll of gauze and had him fixed up in no time at all.

Then she and Dwayne faced the panting cow.

FELICITY DIDN'T SEE DWAYNE WHEN SHE ARRIVED AT GRAPE Seed Ranch. There were surprisingly few cowboys hanging around, and something hung in the still, silent air. As she glanced to the homestead and then back to the pasture where the horses waited, she realized there were no dogs either. No movement. No activity.

It was almost as if the entire ranch had sucked in a breath and held it.

"Hello?" she called.

No one answered.

Her nerves knotted, and she watched as all four horses in the pasture ambled over to the fence and lifted their heads over the top rung.

She couldn't attempt to train Spotlight when her own emotions were so tangled. Decision made, she stepped toward the homestead. She hadn't been properly introduced to Dwayne's parents yet, but there was no time like the present.

She marched down the long, dirt lane and right up the front steps. After knocking, she swept her gaze across the ranch yet again. It was almost eerie, and she startled when the door opened behind her with a *crack!*

She spun to find a honey-haired woman standing there. Dwayne's mother, but Felicity couldn't find a single feature in her face that she'd seen in Dwayne's.

"Hello, dear." She leaned against the doorframe with a healthy smile on her face. She certainly didn't seem concerned about the lack of activity on the ranch before her.

"I'm Felicity Lightburne," she said, stepping forward and extending her hand. "I train the horses here."

They shook hands, and she said, "I know who you are. I'm Maggie Carver, Dwayne's mother." She folded her arms and grinned again.

"Do you—there doesn't seem to be anyone out there." She hooked her thumb over her shoulder toward the ranch.

"Oh, some coyotes broke through the fence in the far-east sector. Our boys are all out there."

"Who is it?" a man called from within the house. He stepped beside his wife, and Felicity found the source of Dwayne's bright blue eyes, his sloped nose, his square jaw.

"You must be Chase Carver." She extended her hand again to the man she'd spoken to on the phone, Dwayne's father who'd hired her. "I'm Felicity."

Chase shook her hand and glanced at his wife. "Dwayne's Felicity?"

Dwayne's Felicity?

She blinked and a sense of vertigo surrounded her.

"Chase." Maggie laughed nervously and nudged her husband. "You hired her to train our horses."

Dwayne's Felicity.

"Oh, of course. Right. How's that coming?"

"Just—fine, sir. Just fine." Felicity fell back a step, her mind reverberating with *Dwayne's Felicity.*

What had he told them about her? Would they be upset about the hand-holding and the Sunday barbeque run?

They didn't seem to be, as they both stood there beaming at her.

"So I guess...I'll get to work." She went down the steps and turned back. "When do you think they'll be back in?"

Maggie squinted into the distance as if she could see them. "Oh, Alyssa just got here a few minutes ago. So probably not for a couple of hours, depending."

On what, she didn't say. Felicity nodded like she knew, though she did not, and walked away from the homestead. Nor did she know who Alyssa was. Or where the far-east sector was.

What she did know was how to get Spotlight to take the rope, so she set out to do that.

A whole mess of cowboys returned just before lunchtime, looking worse for the wear. She'd just put the ropes in the barn and was going to run home to make herself a sandwich, but she turned and searched the crowd of weary faces for the one she wanted to see.

She couldn't find Dwayne.

A buzz lifted into the air, and she twisted to find the source of it. A single ATV made a beeline toward Dwayne's house on the north edge of the homestead property, but she couldn't see if he drove it or not.

"He got cut," a cowboy said to her. "Kurt's gonna get him all doctored up."

Felicity looked into the man's face and found kindness there. "How bad is it?"

"The doc thought it might need stitches. Dwayne'll never do that, so." The cowboy shrugged and moved into the barn, leaving Felicity to argue with herself.

He had his foreman to help him.

He wouldn't want her there.

But she wanted to be there.

She climbed in her car as planned, but instead of heading toward her house for lunch, she did what she'd been doing for the past week and went to Dwayne's. Unsure of what she'd find on the other side of the door, she approached it slowly, nervous and excited at the same time.

Felicity knocked and pushed open the door at the same time. "Hello? Dwayne?"

"Back here," he called from the direction of the bathroom. Male voices murmured, but she couldn't make out any words.

She poked her head into the bathroom to find Dwayne sitting on the closed toilet while Kirk stood slightly behind him, working on the back of his forearm.

"What happened?" she asked, drinking in the full head of sandy brown hair Dwayne possessed. He was just as sexy and good looking without his cowboy hat, and she wanted to run her fingers along the nape of his neck and into that hair.

"He got gouged by chicken wire," Kurt said. "This needs stitches."

"It's fine," Dwayne said, his eyes never leaving Felicity. His gaze burned a path through her bloodstream, and she smiled at him and ducked her head.

"It needs stitches," Kurt repeated.

"I'm not goin' to the hospital."

"You aren't going to fall into another coma."

"Kurt."

"Whatever." The man threw down the medical supplies he'd been holding. He moved toward the door, and Felicity backed into the hall. "Maybe you can talk some sense into him." Kurt gave her a growly look and marched down the hall. A moment later, the back door slammed.

Felicity turned back to Dwayne, her eyebrows raised. "Seems like your foreman is upset with you."

"I'm sure it's not as bad as he says. I can barely feel it anymore." He twisted his arm to look at the wound.

Felicity nodded like she agreed with him and moved around to look at his arm. The wound was at least six inches long, and it did gape open in the middle. She sucked in a breath through her teeth, which created a soft whistle. "Dwayne, I hate to say it, but I think he's right."

Dwayne stood and filled the doorway with his tall frame and broad shoulders. "Would you want to go to a hospital right now?"

She thought of the last time she'd been in a hospital and couldn't conceal the involuntary shudder. "I get it, Dwayne, I do. Maybe an out-patient emergency care clinic?"

He took a step toward her. "You're beautiful. A sight for sore eyes after the morning I've had."

Warmth flooded her, escalating to pure fire when his fingers stuttered over hers before they latched on. He smelled like blood and antiseptic and the wide open range.

"My parents gave me the third degree last night." He chuckled and pressed closer. "My mom was worried we'd gone to Vegas and gotten married."

Felicity laughed but it was a bit forced. "In one afternoon?" She edged into Dwayne's personal space too. "No wonder she was looking at me with such a wide smile."

"When did you see her?"

"This morning, when I got here. The ranch felt...stale. Abandoned. I went over to the homestead."

"I had everyone out in the fields."

"That's what I heard." She ducked her head and touched his arm near his wound. A thrill shot through her, originating from his bare skin. "Gettin' all roughed up."

He brushed her hair back, his fingers trailing down her arm. "Felicity," he said, placing his steady, strong fingers under her chin and gently pushing up.

She looked up at him, the sparks between them morphing into explosions. Without waiting, or asking, or speaking, she lifted up on her toes and pressed her lips to his.

CHAPTER FOURTEEN

Everything Felicity had imagined about kissing Dwayne was true. His right hand trembled as he held her face in his palm, and he tasted like mint and something nutty, and he kissed her like he meant it. Like he'd thought about kissing her too. Like she was his.

He broke the kiss after only a few seconds, and Felicity couldn't quite catch her breath. To hide that fact, she smiled and pressed her forehead to his collarbone.

He wrapped her in his arms and murmured, "That was nice." His voice rumbled through her face and sounded husky, filled with emotion.

"Nice enough to let me take you to an emergency clinic?" She gripped the fabric of his shirt and peered up at him. "It hurts, doesn't it?"

"Little bit." He half-shrugged like it could go either way.

She tipped her head back and let him hold onto her hips while she laughed. He joined in a couple of seconds later, and Felicity enjoyed the sound of their voices—one high and one low—harmonizing.

"So I'll drive you in the mustang."

"Oh, boy," he said, still chuckling. "I don't know if I can get in and out of that thing."

"It's not that bad." She giggled and slipped her hand into his.

"How do you feel about driving a truck?"

"That thing you drive? If you want to end up in the ditch, sure, I'll drive it." They left the house hand-in-hand, and with the sun shining down on them, and the sound of Atlas panting on the front porch, Felicity experienced a moment of happiness —pure happiness—she hadn't expected to feel here in Grape Seed Falls.

———

"ALL RIGHT." FELICITY SIGHED, KEPT BOTH HANDS ON THE steering wheel, and peered through the windshield. "You ready to go in?"

Dwayne hadn't been able to keep his hands to himself. Thankfully, she didn't seem to mind holding his hand. "One thing first." Dwayne met her eye when she looked at him, and he leaned toward her. "How about a kiss for good luck?"

She smiled and dropped her eyes to his mouth. Dwayne kissed her, enjoying the softness of her lips, the butterfly-touch of her fingertips along his jaw, the way she seemed to fill the void that he hadn't even known was in his life.

———

A WEEK PASSED. THE FENCES STAYED FIXED ON THE RANCH. Dwayne's shoulder healed. Payday accepted the bridle, and Felicity kissed him as soon as they entered his house and the door was closed behind them.

Two weeks passed. The summer heat intensified. Dwayne's stitches came out. Spotlight and Payday took a bit, and Felicity had been detailing her neighborhood block party for three solid days before Dwayne asked, "Can I come?"

She'd paused in putting the tack away and glanced over her shoulder. "Yeah, you should come."

"It's on the third, right?" he asked, though he knew her block party was on Monday night. Grape Seed Falls had scheduled their annual fireworks show for Tuesday, the fourth.

"Starts at seven."

"Should I be fashionably late?"

She laughed. "Do you even know how to be late?"

He'd endured two Sundays at church without her, always going to pick her up immediately following the services. They'd gone out to Honey's Hickory three weekends in a row now, and no, he'd never been late.

"I'm sure I can figure it out," he said, hanging up the reins and facing her.

Felicity nudged the door closed with her foot and came toward him. "You could come early if you want. Watch me bake cookies." She slipped her arms around him and gazed up into his face. "Help me get the tables set up and the food out." She shrugged slightly. "If you want."

He wanted to spend all day, every day, with her. Dwayne held her close, bent over to kiss her, fell a little further in love with her. "Let me check with Kurt and make sure I can sneak away. If I can, I'll come early."

She smiled, her mouth only an inch from his, and kissed him again.

A COUPLE OF DAYS LATER, DWAYNE ARRIVED AT THE GRAY AND white brick church on Elberta Street, a sigh hissing from his mouth. He wanted to be here. he just didn't want to be here alone. Not anymore, not when he could be sitting beside Felicity, holding her hand, sharing this part of himself with her.

She hadn't said anything more about her father's death or her fractured faith. The Lord hadn't whispered to Dwayne what to do to help her—if she even needed help. Maybe she didn't. She seemed to enjoy Dwayne's company, liked holding his hand, and kissed him back with as much passion as he poured into his kisses. She appeared happy to be at the ranch, calm with the horses. She laughed at his dumb jokes, and their conversations were sometimes serious and sometimes playful.

Someone knocked on his window, and Dwayne glanced over to find Levi standing in the parking lot. He got out of the truck. "Mornin', Levi."

"I realize now how serious you looked," he said. "I probably interrupted you thinkin' about something important."

"Not really." But now all Dwayne could think about was Heather, and what she might see in Levi. So he was tall, dark, and handsome. Dwayne supposed his sister would like that.

"You still planning to go to Austin at the beginning of October?" Levi asked.

"Of course."

"Want to ride together?"

They'd been making the trip for the horse auction together for a couple of years now. "Sure. If we can take your four-horse trailer."

"As long as you promise not to fill it up yourself." Levi reached the door first and opened it.

Dwayne returned his grin. "Please. I've never bought four horses at once."

"But you wanted to."

"One time." Dwayne made his way toward the right side of the chapel. "And just because I wanted to doesn't mean I did." He sat on the back row, moving all the way against the wall. Sally Stewart already sat at the organ, filling the two-story space with beautiful music that soothed the ragged edges of Dwayne's soul. How Felicity didn't need this in her life, he didn't understand.

Levi sat next to him. "Should I save space for your family?"

An idea shot to the front of Dwayne's mind. "Just Heather." He pulled out his phone and texted his sister about sitting next to him. He stared at the name right under hers, wondering if he could message Felicity too.

Wish you were with me right now, he typed out. Before he could change his mind, he hit send.

Why do I have to sit by you? Heather's message buzzed in his hand, and Dwayne tilted the phone away from Levi, not that the other man was looking. No, he seemed to be scanning the chapel for someone.

You'll see, Dwayne thumbed out and sent before putting his phone away.

"What are you hopin' to get at the auction?" he asked Levi, at a complete loss for how to move the conversation to more personal things.

"Huh?" Levi turned back to him as if he hadn't realized Dwayne was still there. "Oh, I don't know."

"You lookin' for someone?" Dwayne asked when Levi turned and once again surveyed the chapel.

"No." Levi stared forward now, which caused Dwayne to chuckle. With only a few minutes until the service was set to begin, Heather arrived at the end of the pew. Dwayne met her eyes, but she didn't look happy. She stared at him and then Levi, who didn't even seem to notice she'd arrived.

She rolled her eyes, exhaled heavily, and practically stomped down the aisle to where she normally sat with her teacher friends. She bent her head toward Darcy and whispered furiously.

A sense of complete failure flowed through Dwayne, coupled with helplessness. Levi really didn't even act like he knew Heather existed. And who had he been looking for earlier? Dwayne's mind stewed and swirled, getting no closer to any answers.

Pastor Gifford got up and said, "Good morning, brothers and sisters," just as someone touched Dwayne's shoulder. He glanced up to see Felicity standing there. He leapt to his feet, forgetting where he was, and said, "Felicity."

She stood with another woman and a little boy. They looked vaguely familiar to Dwayne, and he'd seen them around a church functions in the past. His heart raced, and a dozen questions ran through his mind.

Felicity flashed a fast smile as Levi said, "Shh."

"Is there room for us?" she whispered.

"Yeah, of course." Dwayne stepped over Levi, who slid against the wall. Felicity entered the pew first, followed by the blonde and her son.

Dwayne put his arm around her shoulder and pulled her close, taking a deep breath of her pineapple and strawberry scent. He was glad she'd come, but his mind rotated around why *he* hadn't been able to influence her to attend church when obviously someone could.

CHAPTER FIFTEEN

The service ended and ten minutes had passed, and Dwayne was almost frantic to leave the church. But he stood half a step behind Felicity, who still hadn't introduced him to her friends.

He'd picked up their names from Levi, who obviously knew them. Capri laughed at everything Levi said, and pieces tumbled into place in Dwayne's mind. He'd been looking for her.

Sourness coated his mouth and he couldn't swallow it away. "Can we go?" he asked Felicity, but she only laughed at something Capri had said and squeezed his hand to get him to stay.

Finally, a lull appeared in Capri and Levi's conversation where Felicity could say, "Capri, this is Dwayne. The man I've been telling you about."

His eyebrows shot up, but he managed to lower them in record time. She shook Capri's hand as Felicity said, "Dwayne, this is Capri. She's my next-door neighbor. She and I have been planning the block party together."

"Oh, right," he said. He couldn't recall the name Capri, but surely Felicity had said it while she'd talked about the party.

"I've heard a lot about you." Capri grinned at him in a knowing way.

"All good," Felicity said.

Dwayne didn't know what to say. Finally, he came up with, "I'm lookin' forward to the block party."

That got Levi talking again, and Dwayne looked at the boy. "What's your name?" he asked.

"Jonah."

"How old are you?"

"Eight."

"So second grade." Dwayne started moving toward the door, and Felicity released his fingers, let him go. Disappointment cut through him, but he couldn't stay in the chapel any longer. Jonah came with him without a word from his mother.

"So you're in second grade," Dwayne said. "My sister teaches third grade. Maybe you'll get her."

"What's her name?"

"Miss Carver."

"She does the pizza box ovens," Jonah said. "I hope I get her."

Dwayne chuckled, though he saw his sister's dark blonde head of hair as she left the church and the laughter died in his throat. "She is a pretty amazing teacher." And a kind person, a good friend. Why didn't Levi notice her?

"So Felicity says you have horses."

"Sure do. She has a couple too."

"Mom takes me riding at Levi's on the weekends." Jonah seemed real proud of himself, and Dwayne reached over and tousled his hair as they moved outside.

"Oh, yeah? Do you like it?"

"Yeah, sure. Mom says I can be a cowboy when I grow up."

Dwayne let the breeze brush his face as he gazed down Elberta Street. The church sat on the corner, with yards and yards of green grass. Homes lined the other side, and everything seemed peaceful.

He'd always loved Grape Seed Falls. Loved riding his bike into town from the ranch and buying candy at the store, or getting a

German sausage from the most popular tourist attraction in town. He'd always known he'd inherit and work the family ranch, and he'd always hoped to have a wife and family of his own to support him as he did.

He hadn't realized how boring his life would be. How ordinary. How mundane.

"The life of a cowboy isn't all that amazing," he said, unsure of where the words had come from. "The hats are great, though." He smiled down at the boy, hoping not to crush his dreams because of a personal revelation about his own cowboy life.

Felicity had spiced up his life, certainly. But a new worry stole through his heart: What if she needed more than the life he could give her?

Branding, plowing, planting, and mending wasn't exciting. He worked hard for a lot of hours. While he made a decent living, there wasn't any pomp or grandeur to what he did.

"My birthday is coming up soon," Jonah said. "Mom said she's gonna get me a cowboy hat."

"That's great," Dwayne said, reminding himself that he'd only met Felicity three weeks ago. He didn't need to be thinking so long-term already. Besides, she'd given no indication that a ranch life wasn't for her.

"I hope she remembers," Jonah said.

"Does she forget stuff a lot?" Dwayne asked, pausing in the shade of an old oak tree.

"Sometimes." He toed the sidewalk, his eyes trained on a dark stain on the ground. "She works a lot and forgets things sometimes."

"What does she do?"

"She's a mechanic."

Surprise moved through Dwayne, and he glanced back at the church, almost willing Felicity to come through the door so they could go. He'd run out of things to talk about with Jonah, and the silence thickened between them.

Finally, Felicity, Capri, and Levi exited, all of them laughing and smiling like they'd just attended a comedy show and not a lecture on being kind to everyone.

"So Capri and Levi want to come to Honey's Hickory with us," Felicity announced when they caught up to Dwayne and Jonah under the tree.

"They do?" Dwayne glanced at Levi, who stood too close to Capri to be casual. He narrowed his eyes at the other cowboy, feeling slighted on behalf of Heather for reasons he couldn't name. He'd never cared who Levi went out with before, and he couldn't figure out how he felt.

"That's okay, isn't it?" Felicity asked, her smile slipping from her face.

His brain felt stuffed full and too slow, the way it had for months and years after his injury. He needed more time to process. Less eyes looking at him while he did. He couldn't think of a reason why he didn't want Capri and Levi to come with them to Honey's, other than that he just wanted to be alone with Felicity.

"Yeah, that's okay," he said, though it wasn't. He wished he knew why it wasn't, why he felt like he was being disloyal to his sister, why Felicity could come to church when Capri asked and not when he did.

FELICITY SENSED SOMETHING WAS OFF-KILTER IN DWAYNE. HE'D shown signs of restlessness in the chapel after the service, and then he'd left with Jonah. She supposed she should've answered his text before showing up in the chapel. Or let him know she was coming that morning and asked him to save her a seat.

He'd definitely been surprised to see her at church, and she'd seen a flicker of emotion enter his expression. What emotion, she hadn't been able to name—and she'd tried during the hour-long sermon.

She wanted to feel something at church. Feel loved. Feel like God knew she was there, that she was trying.

She'd felt nothing but the weight of Dwayne's arm around her shoulders.

"What's wrong?" she finally asked as they left Grape Seed Falls in the rear-view mirror.

"Nothing," he said. But he kept both hands on the steering wheel when he normally threaded his trembling fingers through hers.

"You're gripping the steering wheel like you're trying to crush it."

His fingers relaxed. "I'm—Capri seems nice."

Felicity brightened. "She's great. My first friend in Grape Seed Falls."

"I'm not your friend?" His glance was filled with flirt, and she giggled before reaching for his hand and prying it from the wheel.

"My first girlfriend, who someone who doesn't wear a cowboy hat and boots to work."

"Levi likes her." His voice grated through his throat.

She frowned and tried to find the meaning in those three words. "I suppose so," she said. "They were flirting a little."

"A lot," Dwayne said.

"Do *you* like her?" Felicity asked.

"Of course not. I didn't even know her name."

"Why are you upset about them flirting then?"

He sighed, and Felicity knew she'd found the cause of his negative vibes. Relief poured through her that it was an outside issue, something she didn't need to analyze and fix inside herself.

"My sister...likes Levi." He turned toward her, ignoring the road completely. "You can't tell anyone. Heather would kill me."

"Your sister likes Levi." The words felt like lead in her gut. "I didn't know, Dwayne. I swear."

"She's been going out to his stable to ride on Fridays." He waved his hand as if performing a magic spell. "To...see him, I guess. Get him to notice her. Or something."

Nerves danced in Felicity's stomach. "Capri's been taking Jonah to ride on Fridays too." And now Felicity knew why. She couldn't help a quick laugh. "Do you think Levi knows of his effect on women?"

Dwayne shook his head. "The guy's clueless."

"Well, most men are," Felicity said.

"Hey," Dwayne protested.

"I'm just saying—before Heather told you, did you know *why* she went riding on Fridays?"

"No."

"And you still don't even really know why she does it."

"I do. She—"

"You just said 'to get him to notice her. Or something.'" She mimicked his hand-flapping. "Sometimes a person will go to great lengths to get noticed."

He cut a glance at her. "Are we still talkin' about Heather and Levi?"

Felicity wasn't really sure. If she wanted him to be her boyfriend—and maybe something more—she'd have to tell him everything eventually. She gazed out the passenger window, her hand still in his but her thoughts far away.

"Just my mother again." She pushed the memories, the hurt, away.

His hand tightened on hers, further grounding her. "Well, she's not a man."

A burst of laughter exploded from her mouth. "I guess you're right." She snuggled into his arm, inhaling the scent of the laundry detergent caught in his shirt. "I guess women can be as dense of men."

"I reckon so." He cleared his throat and shifted in his seat. "Like how you came to church with Capri when I've asked every week for a month."

Felicity's heart froze. Her lungs, too. "I—" But she had no explanation. She hadn't even realized what she'd done. The emotion she'd seen flicker across his face made sense now. So did the white-knuckle driving. It *had* been about her, and something she needed to fix.

"I—I don't know what to say. I'm sorry, Dwayne."

"Did you like church?"

"Not especially." She hated how the words sounded coming out of her mouth, but they were true.

"It was an interesting topic."

Felicity had barely heard a word of the sermon, and she didn't want to admit that. She'd been thinking about Dwayne during church, and she held that close to the vest too.

"I suppose so."

"Maybe you'll just need to keep coming until you hear something you like."

"Maybe." Her tone clearly suggested her non-committal attitude, and thankfully, Dwayne reached over and turned up the volume on the radio.

"I love this song," he said about the country song playing through the speakers. Felicity listened to his beautiful voice sing along to the lyrics, more peace flowing through her now than she'd felt in the chapel.

Her throat narrowed. She wasn't sure why God had shut her out, but as Dwayne crossed over the city limits of Cypress, where Honey's Hickory waited, she had the distinct impression that *she* was the one holding the door between her and the Lord closed.

CHAPTER SIXTEEN

Felicity got out of Dwayne's truck like she had for the past month. The blue sky was the same, with the addition of a handful of puffy, white clouds. The line in front of Honey's was the same.

The scent of smoked brisket hit her in the gut like a swift kick. Her memory flooded with moments she'd spent with her father while he prepared the brisket, got the hickory chips prepared, and sliced the finished product. All she could think was, *He's gone. I'll never taste his brisket again. He's gone.*

Gone.

Gone.

Her head hurt, and she couldn't take a breath. Dwayne said something, but she couldn't decipher the words. Tears pricked her eyes and flowed down her face without her permission, suddenly just there. So many of them.

She was aware of him moving her away from the crowd, not toward it, but she honestly didn't know how she was walking.

Grief rolled over her, again and again, and Dwayne finally wrapped her in his arms and held on tight. She fisted her fingers in his shirt and cried until she was spent. She couldn't understand what had just happened. How was she supposed to explain it to him?

Every cell in her body felt like it was about to combust, and her head felt so hot, so hot. Combined with the sun and Dwayne's body heat, she was sticky and sweaty in all the wrong places.

Almost as if by magic, her throat cleared and she drew in a deep breath. What had been crazed before calmed. Felicity stepped out of Dwayne's embrace and tried to put herself back together, at least physically.

He said nothing, but he didn't look away from her, not even for a moment. He liked his unwavering attention and hated it at the same time.

"Sorry," she muttered, wondering if today would be filled with apologies.

"I don't much feel like barbeque today," he said, finally breaking his gaze away from her and focusing on the sky. "Want to try something else?"

She nodded and wiped her hands down her face, finding black makeup on her fingers. "I just need—"

"Restroom right behind you." He nodded, and she escaped, wondering when she'd started to rely on him so much. Wondering when she'd started falling in love with him.

Felicity looked at herself in the bathroom mirror and found a freak staring back. Her chin trembled, but she pulled the emotion back. She'd cried twice in front of him now, and she considered it a miracle that he was still around.

Fear struck her right in the breastbone. Maybe he'd be gone when she emerged from the restroom.

Don't be ridiculous, she told herself. After all, she was the one who ran away when things got hard. Wasn't that what her mother had accused her of?

You can't just run away to the cabin because you don't want to celebrate Christmas with us.

But it wasn't about celebrating Christmas with her mother and brothers. It was about celebrating Christmas without her father.

Fine. Just go. Run away to some other ranch.

Her mother's final words to her screamed through her mind, her soul. She hadn't run away to Grape Seed Ranch. She had plans to return to Marysville and the family ranch for Labor Day. Gordon and Parker knew she was coming. They'd promised to take her to the Fall Festival, make homemade ice cream, and go riding through the hills they'd all grown up exploring.

Just thinking about her brothers made her smile, and that erased some of the agony from her features. She turned on the cold water and washed her hands, running them down her face while they were still wet.

Help me, she prayed. She wanted to finish the sentence, tell God exactly what she needed, but she found she couldn't.

Help me about summed it all up.

DWAYNE RECOGNIZED A PANIC ATTACK WHEN HE SAW ONE. First, he'd experienced more of them than he wanted to admit. Second, Felicity wore her emotions so close to the surface that he'd practically seen it coming from the moment they'd left Grape Seed Falls behind.

He paced outside the restrooms, wondering if she'd somehow come out and he hadn't seen her. She'd been inside for a while now, and while his stomach cramped from hunger, it was really angry at him for not knowing how to help her when she so clearly needed it.

All of his petitions to the Lord on the subject had gone unanswered, and in the end Dwayne had to depend on himself. He'd gotten her away from the restaurant, the prying eyes. He'd held her close and tight, as when he'd experienced his anxiety attacks, having somewhere contained had provided him with the safety and security he lacked.

She'd quieted relatively quickly, but Dwayne was mostly concerned about how to prevent future attacks. Frustration boiled through him. She'd shared some things about herself and her life with him. Some deeply personal things, he knew.

But he also knew she hadn't shared everything. And with Felicity, he wanted everything.

Do I push her? he wondered. He turned, and there she was.

He swallowed and stuffed his hands in his pockets. "Hey." His voice came out kind and small and he tacked a smile onto the word.

Not wanting to be awkward or add to her burden, he unpocketed one of his hands and reached for hers. "Should we go? I know this little pancake house on the other side of town. They have the best cinnamon roll pancakes on the planet. They serve them with icing instead of syrup." He took a breath, hoping he didn't sound too cheerful or too dismissive of what had just happened.

"And I believe you mentioned something about a love of bacon." He grinned at her, bent down and touched the brim of his hat to hers. "And they have thick-slab bacon they cure in-house."

A spark of interest entered her eyes. They turned glassy a moment later. "You're a really great guy," she whispered. "I don't deserve someone like you."

"Don't say that." He wasn't all that great, and she deserved the best. He turned and gently led her back to the truck. Once they were settled inside, with the air conditioner blowing, he asked, "So, do you have panic attacks often?"

She stared at her hands, the embarrassment streaming from her and filling the air between them. "No. That was...unexpected. The smell of brisket reminded me of my father, and I just sort of...lost it." She looked at him then, her expression open and honest and raw. "It's odd. We've been coming here for weeks, and I've been okay. Today, it's...not okay. I just...I just miss him so much."

"I know you do." He lifted her knuckles to his lips. "I'm sorry, sweetheart."

Her face was a bit blotchy, but when she smiled she was still an absolute vision. He leaned over at the same time he pushed his hat back. "I'd do anything to make you happy," he whispered just before lightly touching his lips to hers.

He straightened, his insides quaking at the admission, at the depth of his feelings for her, at the way he'd expressed himself.

She snuggled into his side like she had on the drive over, and he repositioned his hat back into its proper place. "I'd love some of those pancakes, and as much bacon as they'll legally allow me to eat."

Happiness burst through him. "I don't think there's a legal limit on bacon consumption in the state of Texas."

"Thank goodness." She sighed and closed her eyes, which prompted Dwayne to drive as slowly as he could to the pancake house across town if only to keep her at his side, extend this peaceful moment with her, for as long as possible.

Dwayne arrived at Felicity's the following afternoon about two o'clock. He found her in the kitchen, singing along loudly to pop music he'd never heard before. She added vanilla to the bowl and switched the mixer on before dropping in two eggs.

He admired the swing of her hips as she added dance moves to the song, and he burst out laughing when she picked up the rubber spatula and used it as a microphone.

She spun toward him, dropping the utensil and silencing her voice. Her fingers fumbled over the countertop until she located a remote and muted the music. His laughter filled the silence, and Felicity stalked toward him with a flirtatious smile on her face.

"Hey, there," he said, receiving her into his arms easily. "Why'd you stop? I liked that."

"We don't all have your musical talent."

"Your dance moves are far superior than mine."

"I've never even seen your dance moves." She slid her hands to his shoulders, and he started to sway with her to music only he could hear.

"Mm." His eyes drifted closed as she pressed into him and laid her cheek against his chest. He began to hum, and today felt so different than only twenty-four hours ago. "How're you feeling today?" he asked. "I missed seeing you at the ranch this morning."

"You made Spotlight wear the bridle, didn't you?"

"'Course." He noticed that she didn't answer his question about how she was feeling.

"I hope you didn't eat a big lunch."

"Why's that?" He dipped his head so he could trace his lips along her ear.

She giggled and pushed against his chest. "Because I need you to be my taste-tester." She skipped over to the kitchen counter and lifted the paddle attachment. After collecting a spoon from the drawer in the island, she scooped up a bite of cookie dough and extended it toward him.

He joined her at the island and let her feed him the dough. It was one of the sexiest things he'd ever done, and he couldn't look away from her dark eyes. Lightning struck between them, and Dwayne had the distinct impression that there would be many storms ahead for him and Felicity. But he wanted to weather them all right at her side.

She scraped her bottom lip with her teeth and said, "So?"

He almost choked but managed to swallow the sweet treat without incident. "Tastes amazing."

She grinned and started scooping the dough. "How are you with a knife?"

"Decent. My mother wanted me to be able to take care of myself."

Felicity nodded toward a cutting board and chef's knife. "Oh, yeah?"

He picked up the knife. "I think when I turned twenty-one, still lived in the homestead, and didn't have a girlfriend, she realized I needed some culinary skills." He chuckled, remembering the "summer of sauces" he'd endured.

Felicity got out a rainbow of bell peppers and set him to

making rings she was planning to sauté for the bratwursts a neighbor down the street would be grilling. He told her about the months of cooking lessons his mother had given him, the "week of breads," and "month of salads."

"I like your mom more and more." She bumped him with her hip, and Dwayne had never felt as comfortable with a woman as he did with Felicity. He tried to put a cap on his swelling feelings, but they grew and grew.

He chopped while she baked cookies, while one batch finished, and she scooped another. His thoughts circled around starting a conversation of their past relationships. She'd hinted that she hadn't had a lot of boyfriends, but she'd never asked him about his romantic history.

When Dwayne finally ran out of peppers, he turned to the stove to start the fire to melt the butter. "Felicity," he said, his heart fluttering the way his fingers did. "I have something I want to tell you."

The timer went off on the second batch of cookies, and she silenced it with a quick look in his direction. She pulled the tray out of the oven and silenced the timer. "What's that?"

"So, you said you hadn't had a lot of boyfriends." He picked up a handful of peppers and set them in the sizzling butter. After adding a swirl of salt and several shakes of pepper, he faced her. "I haven't dated a lot in recent years, but before that, I was engaged."

Her eyes widened and her mouth opened into a cute little O. "Engaged. Wow."

"Her name was Serenity, and well, we were together for a year before I proposed. Engaged for two after that." He didn't want to get tangled in all the memories. All the should've's and could've's. "In the end, she couldn't go through with it." He ducked his head as his heart belted out a warning for him to stop opening himself up so wide. After all, it didn't want to get shattered all over again.

"Why not?" Felicity asked.

Dwayne picked up the wooden spoon she'd gotten out for him

and turned back to the softening peppers. He stirred them, the words clogged behind his vocal chords.

"You don't have to say." Her hand landed on his bicep, somehow giving him strength and courage.

"She...she found ranch life too slow." He looked at Felicity, his fear finally out. "I...I worry about that with you, too."

She searched his face, shock traveling over hers. "Dwayne, how can you even think that?"

He shrugged one shoulder, his insecurities rushing through him like water over a steep drop.

"I grew up on a ranch," Felicity said. "I love ranch life."

Her sincerity calmed some of his fears. "Maybe I'm being ridiculous," he said quietly. "It's just...I never saw that coming from Serenity either. Her father owns a ranch on the other side of the Hammond orchards."

"The Rhodes?"

He nodded, his focus singular on the peppers, which were coming along nicely. "She left Hill Country completely after we broke up." Which Dwayne was extremely happy about. If she hadn't, he was sure it would've taken longer than a few years to start dating again.

"I heard she's going to law school," Dwayne said. "Lives in a high-rise in Dallas or something." He pushed the peppers around. "These are done. Where do you want them?"

She busied herself getting out a plate and lining it with a paper towel. He slid the peppers onto it and put another slab of butter in the still-hot pan and added another handful of vegetables.

"So now you know," he said. "I wanted you to know."

"Thank you, Dwayne." She spoke with that same soft, reverent tone he adored.

"So," he said in a stronger voice. "Anything like that in your past?"

She laughed and joined him at the stove. "Not even close."

"You've had boyfriends, I'm sure."

"One or two."

Dwayne stopped cooking and looked at her. "One or two? That's all?" Impossible. Someone as beautiful as her? Surely she had men asking her out all the time.

"I...spent a lot of time on the ranch, with the horses."

"All right." He cooked vegetables while she boiled pasta for a salad. The hours passed easily with casual conversation and flirty touches. Finally, she deemed everything ready and asked him to get the tables set up on the driveway.

Before he slipped out the front door to do as she asked, he drew her into his embrace and kissed her. "I had a great afternoon." He smiled down at her.

"Just wait until the party starts."

Dwayne stayed behind the scenes during the block party. Felicity had changed into a flirty pair of black shorts and a lemon-yellow blouse, leaving her cowgirl hat behind. She laughed and spoke with her friends and neighbors, and Dwayne liked the non-cowgirl version of her as much as the ranch woman he'd first met.

She finally dragged him off her front steps and out to meet the community she'd become part of over the past several weeks. It seemed important to her that he know them, so he shook hands and made small talk.

He knew a few of the families, as they were generational Grape Seed Falls residents. He stuck close to a man only a year or two older than him, a Rick Dunham.

"You still makin' those custom saddles?" Dwayne asked.

"Yep." He served himself some of Felicity's pasta salad. "Your dad used to buy one from us every year."

Dwayne's birthday was coming up, and he suddenly knew what he wanted. "How long does it take to make a saddle like that?"

Rick sized him up. "Depends on what you want."

"I'm training up a horse right now, and I think I'd like a saddle for him."

"I like a cowboy who thinks the saddle is for his horse and not him." Rick grinned at him. "Come by the shop, and bring your horse."

"Oh, Payday isn't ready for a trailer yet."

"Almost," Felicity said, sidling up to the conversation.

"You think so?" Dwayne looked down at her to see if she was serious.

"Why? Where you takin' him?" She leaned closer. "Surely you're not going to board him with Levi."

Dwayne sucked in a breath and said, "No. Rick's gonna make Payday a custom saddle."

Felicity whistled as she twisted the top on a hot dog bag that had been left open. "He'll be the fanciest horse at the ranch."

"One can hope," Dwayne said with a smile.

CHAPTER SEVENTEEN

July passed in one long wave of heat. Payday made good progress so that by the time August dawned, Dwayne could put a saddle on him without incident. It wasn't the custom-made one from Rick, as Dwayne hadn't gotten Payday into the trailer quite yet.

Spotlight was coming along a little slower, but Felicity hadn't exhibited any frustration over the issue.

In fact, since her panic attack just before the Fourth of July holiday, she hadn't shown any more tears, any more grief, any more sorrow over her father's death. Dwayne suspected she'd been sharing that part of her life with Capri, and that made his heart hurt. But he didn't know how to make her share with him.

He made sure he was in the pasture or training ring before her, so he could greet her with a smile each morning. They shared lunch—and more than a few kisses—every weekday. And she'd started coming to church with him, too.

They'd never spoken about the sermons they heard. Dwayne simply wanted her to be able to feel the power and spirit of the Lord for herself, and he often needed time to make sense of Pastor Gifford's words for himself anyway.

It didn't really matter what the pastor said. Dwayne had always appreciated the feeling of simply being in the church. The music more than anything the pastor said soothed his soul, and Dwayne just wanted Felicity to experience a part of that comfort.

The second Sunday in August, Felicity slid onto the bench a few minutes after the pastor had stood to start. That was her usual routine. Arrive just a bit late and slip out as soon as the sermon ended. Dwayne didn't mind. He showed up ten minutes early and listened to Sally play the organ, feeding his spirit in that short time.

"I'm going to Marysville after the sermon today," she whispered, keeping her eyes on the pulpit up front. "Do you want to come with me?"

"Yeah, of course." Dwayne's heart started pounding, as he'd never met her mom or her brothers. Felicity had talked about them a lot, claimed to be in constant contact with her oldest brother, Gordon, and Dwayne knew there was some bad blood between her and her mother.

"Why are you going home today?" he asked.

"It's my brother's birthday." She tucked her hand into his elbow and crossed her legs. Today she wore one of her three dresses—the navy blue one with bright pink flamingos stitched into the fabric. "I wasn't going to go home until Labor Day, but Parker called and said Gordon would really like it if I was there. And it's only an hour and a half, so...."

Which gave Dwayne two and a half hours to figure out how to meet his girlfriend's family.

FELICITY FELT BETTER DRIVING BESIDE DWAYNE THAN SHE HAD in almost a year. They'd been getting along so well that when Parker had called that morning, Felicity had immediately agreed to come for dinner.

Parker and Gordon knew about Dwayne, but her mom didn't.

So the closer to Marysville the truck went, the bigger the pit in Felicity's stomach became.

"Remember how I said our ranch wasn't as nice as yours?" she asked as he passed the "Welcome to Marysville!" sign.

He cut a glance at her. "Are you nervous?"

"A little," she admitted.

"You've told me all about your ranch," he said. "And your family. It's going to be fine." He squeezed her hand. "I *want* to meet them."

Of course he did. Dwayne was a good man, and Felicity struggled to believe she deserved someone like him. Someone who had such great faith. Who never seemed to get tired, though she'd seen him take a twenty minute nap during lunch. Who never said a bad word about anyone. Felicity had never had much drama in her life either—except with her mother—and she found herself praying that everything would go smoothly as Dwayne made the final turn and pointed the truck down the road where her family's ranch waited.

"It's on the right up there." She nodded as if he wouldn't be able to see the huge arch announcing the Bluebonnet Ranch and Family Farm. "My father carved that sign, and he insisted we get up there every fall to stain the bluebonnets." She spoke in a quiet voice, fully expecting the memories to smother her the way they had in the past.

But they didn't. A smile carved its way across her face, and she continued with, "He loved bluebonnets. Used to give them to me and my mother every year for our birthdays. He grows them in the back corner of the yard. You'll see."

Dwayne simply squeezed his hand and took a long look at the sign.

"Doesn't look like my brothers have done the staining yet." She noticed the faded flowers on the arch.

"That's a big arch," Dwayne said as they passed underneath it. "How did you get up there to stain it?"

Images flowed through Felicity's mind like the lavender honey her mother loved. "Daddy used to rent the fire truck."

"You can rent a fire truck?" He came to a stop in the driveway of her childhood home, and Felicity's vocal chords seized.

She shrugged though she wanted to tell him that the former fire chief was Daddy's brother, so getting access to it hadn't been all that hard. But the wave of homesickness assaulting her kept her silent. And when Gordon stepped onto the front porch, Felicity launched herself out of the truck with a laugh.

She ran up to the steps and took them two at a time, saying, "Happy birthday, Gordon!"

He chuckled as he caught her around the waist. "What are you doin' here?"

"Parker said to come." Felicity beamed at her oldest brother, who she'd always gotten along with.

"And you brought your boyfriend."

Felicity sucked a breath in through her teeth, which made a whistling sound. "Um, yes, Dwayne came with me."

He got out of the truck and Felicity watched him take an extra moment to squeeze his right fingers into a ball. He closed his eyes for a long second, and then put a smile on his face as he walked toward the porch a little less enthusiastically than she had.

"So he's not your boyfriend?" Gordon asked, his grin stuck in place and his lips barely moving.

"He...is, I guess."

"So how are you gonna introduce him?"

Felicity gave her brother a glare and joined Dwayne as he reached the top of the steps. "Dwayne, this is my little brother, Gordon. He's older than Parker." She glanced at Parker as he came through the front door too.

"You made it." He grinned and gave her a quick hug. "And you must be Dwayne."

"She was just introducing him." Gordon flashed her a wicked smile.

"And Parker," Felicity said with a heavy dose of *stop-it-right-now-*

Gordon. No wonder she hadn't dated much while she worked on this ranch. "He's the youngest. Guys, this is Dwayne Carver, my boss at Grape Seed Ranch, and my boyfriend."

She lifted her gaze to watch him, and he was as flawless as ever. He smiled and said hello, shook each brother's hand, and returned to her side, where he slipped his shaking hand along her back before it settled on her hip.

"Where's Mom?" she asked.

"Napping," Gordon said, his dark features turning somber.

"I just woke her up," Parker said quickly, shooting a glance at his brother. "She's comin'."

Felicity looked between them. "Mom is taking a nap?" She'd never known her mother to nap, ever. Even when she'd been up all night with Felicity when she'd had the stomach flu, her mother did not lie down during the day.

"Too much to be done," she'd say, and she'd look perfect getting the laundry done, the dishes clean, and dinner on the table. Felicity had hated being in the house with her mother. Not enough fresh air and too many expectations.

"She hasn't been feeling well," Gordon said.

"Gordon," Parker admonished. He looked at Felicity with their mother's lighter eyes, her fairer hair poking out the bottom of his cowboy hat. "She's fine."

"Felicity isn't stupid," Gordon argued. "She'll take one look at Mom and know she's not well."

Fear doused Felicity's lungs in icy water. "What's wrong with her?"

"They're not sure," Parker said, switching his gaze back to Gordon. "Could be a cold."

Gordon rolled his eyes, and Felicity realized they'd been having this argument a lot. "Well, let's go in. I suppose she's why you made such a big deal out of me makin' brisket for my own birthday." He opened the door and entered the house, Parker trailing him.

"She loves brisket."

"It's *my* birthday." Gordon's voice carried back to them.

"I made you your favorite ice cream cake, so stop complaining," Parker said.

Felicity giggled and glanced up at Dwayne. "My brothers."

"They're nice." He followed her into the house, which hadn't changed at all, except for the air held a hint of stuffiness along with the scent of smoking meat. Her stomach growled, but she needed to find her mother first.

"Momma?" She laced her fingers through Dwayne's and held on tight. He seemed to know she needed additional anchoring, because he squeezed and stayed only inches behind her.

"She's in here," Gordon called from the kitchen.

Felicity drew in a deep breath and went around the wall that separated the formal living room in the front of the house from the kitchen and great room in the back.

Her mother sat in her favorite armchair, her normally curled and quaffed, sandy brown hair matted on one side and poking out weirdly on the other. "Hey, Mom."

"Felicity." She got to her feet quickly and started forward. Her step seemed unsure, and Parker abandoned his task of setting the table and lunged for her, latching onto her arm to steady her. Her eyes seemed as sharp as ever, and though it took precious seconds for her to find her footing, she didn't miss Dwayne's hand in Felicity's.

Felicity embraced her mom and drew back, her hands still on her mother's shoulders. "How are you?"

"Fine, fine." She patted her hair. "These boys pamper me too much."

"It's Gordon's birthday," Parker said. "We normally just eat grilled cheese sandwiches after church."

"Too much to do," Gordon added from the kitchen. He took the aluminum foil off a large pan, a burst of steam lifting toward the ceiling. The smell of hickory-smoked brisket made another wave of homesickness roll over Felicity.

"Time to eat," he announced.

"Mom," Felicity said. "This is Dwayne Carver, my boyfriend. Dwayne, my mother." No need to mention the boss part this time. Her mom probably wouldn't like that, and Felicity saw no need to give her mom anything to lecture about.

"My pleasure to meet you, ma'am." Dwayne's bass voice could turn anyone's head, but as he extended his hand for her mother to shake, she didn't even flinch.

Her gaze drank in Dwayne from the top of his cowboy hat to the soles of his boots. Once, then twice.

"Hurry up and shake the man's hand, Momma," Gordon said. "I'm starving."

"The pleasure is mine," Momma finally said, putting her hand in Dwayne's. He seemed to know that he needed to treat her like royalty, because he lifted her hand to his mouth and pressed a kiss to the backside of her palm.

"Let's eat." Relief ran rampant through her, and Felicity nudged Dwayne toward the table Parker had arranged. "Who's saying grace?"

"Gordon," Parker said at the same time Gordon said, "Parker."

"It's my birthday," he said again.

Parker scowled and said the prayer. He ended it with, "And thank you for allowing Felicity and Dwayne to be with us. Bless them to travel safely back to Grape Seed Falls. Amen."

Her mom didn't even wait for the final echo of the amen to settle before she said, "Tell us all about this other ranch. Do you work there too, Dwayne?"

CHAPTER EIGHTEEN

F elicity's hair blew in the breeze, and she gathered it into her palm and held it against her shoulder. Dwayne wandered a few paces ahead of her, his fingertips brushing the delicate tops of the wild bluebonnets her father had cultivated.

He'd answered all her mother's questions with smiles and happiness in his voice. When Momma had shown disdain at Felicity dating her boss, Dwayne had reached for Felicity's hand and squeezed it. Said, "I own the ranch. I'm not really her boss," and moved on.

Though he most certainly was her boss, because he owned the ranch. It had never been an issue between them, and Felicity wasn't going to make it one simply because her mother didn't approve.

Ahead of her, Dwayne lifted his head and gazed into the distance. She approached and slipped her arm through his. "It's beautiful here," she said.

He glanced down at her, a quick smile on his lips. He was handsome and magnificent, and Felicity felt her heart swelling with love for him. He bent, plucked a flower, and lovingly threaded it behind her ear.

"You're beautiful." His whisper sent shivers across her shoulders, and she received his tender kiss willingly. She couldn't believe she was standing in her father's favorite spot, kissing a man for all to see. She felt like she and Dwayne were the only two people on earth, and the only witness to their love was the blue sky and the fluttering breeze.

No matter what, Felicity had never felt as strongly for anyone as she felt for Dwayne. He tucked her into his side and they looked out over the fence at the waving grasses and another field of bluebonnets. He sighed, a happy, contented sound that infused Felicity's soul with peace.

"Felicity," he said, his voice choked with emotion.

"Yeah?"

"I think I'm falling in love with you." He didn't look at her, didn't knead her closer, didn't say anything else.

A smile drifted across her face and she twisted to look at him. "Let's go home."

FELICITY THOUGHT A LOT ABOUT WHAT DWAYNE HAD SAID OVER the course of the next couple of weeks. She was certain she was falling in love with him too, but she didn't quite know what to do about it. Training horses and learning how to immunize cattle seemed to be enough for now, but she wondered when Dwayne would want more.

He'd hinted that she was the one who would want more, but she kept searching her soul, and it was content with ranch life. No, not just ranch life. Ranch life with Dwayne.

She couldn't believe she'd called Grape Seed Falls "home" and had easily left her family's ranch in Marysville. Sure, the homesickness had hit her once or twice, but she didn't want to return to Bluebonnet Farm to live, to work the land, to train horses. Not anymore.

"There you are." Capri stopped on Felicity's back steps and cocked her hip. "I've been knocking for ten minutes."

"You have not." Felicity laughed and watched Whiskers streak out of the house as if Capri would stop him and shut him back in the spare bedroom. "The screen's open. I haven't heard a single knock."

Capri collapsed into the patio chair beside Felicity. "Fine. I just walked in."

"Busy day?" Felicity noticed Capri's grease-stained fingernails and wispy ponytail.

"Two tourists broke down on their way through town." Capri sighed, leaned back, and closed her eyes. "Somehow it's my fault if I don't have their specific fan belt in stock." She tilted her head toward Felicity and cracked one eye. "Good money, though."

"Hmm." Felicity sipped her iced tea. "Where's Jonah tonight?"

"Down at Zack's. Birthday party."

Felicity eyed her friend. "So you're here, hoping I'll order pizza. Is that right?"

"I'm surprised you haven't already." Capri laughed, the sound fading quickly. "So, how are you and Dwayne?"

"Great." Felicity sighed happily without meaning to.

"Oh, that good, huh?" Capri giggled and opened her eyes to look at Felicity. She searched her face for something, but Felicity didn't know what.

She finally asked, "What?"

"Do you think I'll be able to find someone like Dwayne?"

Felicity caught the worry in her friend's eyes, the desperation and hope in her tone. "What about Levi? Why'd you two stop going out?"

A flash of pain flitted across Capri's face. "He wasn't interested."

"He said that?"

"Right to my face." Capri gripped the armrests on the chair. "He seemed...I don't know. Embarrassed about it. Or at least sorry."

Felicity reached over and patted Capri's hand. "Maybe you shouldn't be looking for a cowboy."

"Then I should probably leave the state of Texas." Capri let her words settle for two heartbeats and then she burst out laughing. Felicity joined her, because it seemed like every man in Texas either was a cowboy or a football player. Or wanted to be a cowboy or a football player.

"Besides," Capri said. "I like cowboys. My husband was a cowboy."

Felicity didn't know what to say, so she kept her mouth shut.

"You seem happy," Capri said after several minutes.

"You know what?" Felicity watched the shadows length over her backyard as the sun continued to set. "I am." She looked at Capri, a bit of her fear coming out in her voice when she said, "I think this is the happiest I've ever been."

Capri said, "I'm so happy for you, honey," leaving Felicity to wonder why she was allowing her worries and fears to dampen her joy.

"Now, what about that pizza...."

DWAYNE GLANCED UP FROM HIS LAPTOP WHEN JINX BARKED. Atlas didn't move from his position on the couch, so whoever had come to his house wasn't a threat.

"Who is it, boy?" he asked.

A few moments later, a light knock sounded on his door. Not a cowboy's fist. He left his browser open to the horses he'd been scouting and answered the door.

"Felicity." Surprise colored his tone. She hadn't said she was coming out to the ranch this Saturday morning. He kept one hand on the door and leaned into the frame. "What are you doin' here?"

"I'm riding Lucy this morning, and she wanted Payday to come with us."

His eyebrows went up. "You think he's ready for that?"

"You've had a saddle on him for weeks. It's time to ride 'em, cowboy." She gave him the sexiest smile he'd ever seen, and he wanted to kiss it off her mouth.

"All right," he said instead, turning back to the kitchen table where he'd been working. "Let me finish this up."

She followed him into the kitchen and took the only other seat at the table. "What are you doing?"

Dwayne suddenly didn't want to tell her. A squirrel of embarrassment scampered through him. "Um, looking at horses." He closed the laptop with a definitive *clap!* "I'm ready to go now. I can finish later."

Felicity didn't move. "What kind of horse are you looking at?"

Dwayne considered her, the blaze in her dark eyes, the slightly standoffish way she folded her arms. "Would you be upset if I bought another horse?"

"I think you should break the two wild ones you already have."

"What if the horse was already broken?" Because the bay he'd been looking at was picture-perfect online. Beautiful markings, saddle-ready, an old ranch hand.

"You can do whatever you want with your money," she said. "It's your ranch." She took a few steps toward the front door before turning back to him. "Is this mystery horse at the auction you're attending in a couple of weeks? The one I'm not invited to?" The venom wasn't hard to find in her voice. She hadn't even tried to mask it.

"Ah, so that's why you're mad."

"I'm not mad, Dwayne."

He followed her to the front door and pushed against it so she couldn't escape. "Why didn't you say you wanted to go to the auction?"

She gave him a great view of her new hatband—this one made of purple glass beads and white chunks of rock. She'd told him once that she made all her hatbands, and he liked that each was unique but also seemed to fit her.

"You seemed excited to go with Levi," she said.

"I like going with Levi," Dwayne admitted. "We've gone together for a few years now. He knows horses, and I trust his opinion." He ran his fingers down her bare arm, satisfied when she received his fingers between hers. "You're welcome to come with us."

She lifted her chin and looked him dead in the eye. "Right. Me in between the two of you. I don't think so."

"You know horses, and I trust your opinion." Dwayne hoped she didn't think that was the reason he hadn't invited her. He honestly hadn't even thought about taking her with him. Why hadn't he?

Because the trip was already planned, he told himself. Before Felicity even showed up on the ranch.

"Felicity, would you like to come to the horse auction with me?" He lowered his head and brushed his lips along her cheek. "There's plenty of room. Levi has a horse trailer that holds four." He held her against him and kissed her neck. "Maybe you'll find a horse you want."

"I can't afford a horse," she whispered, her hands moving to his shoulders and holding on.

"I'll buy you one," he promised.

"You're not buying me a horse." She giggled and pushed away from him. "Don't be ridiculous."

"It's not ridiculous. Your birthday is coming up."

"In December." She cocked her head and shook it. "No, you go to your horse auction with Levi. Maybe you can find out why he told Capri he wasn't interested in her."

Dwayne's curiosity shot toward the heavens. "He did?"

"That's what she said."

His brain started working overtime. If Levi wasn't dating Capri anymore, maybe Heather had a chance....

Of course, his sister probably already knew all about Levi and Capri and anything that was said. She didn't need Dwayne to play matchmaker. Still, Felicity's suggestion to ask Levi about the women in his life seemed like a very good one.

Twenty minutes later, he put his foot in the stirrup. His pulse thumped a little roughly, but Payday held completely still. "Good boy," Dwayne said as he pushed himself up and pulled himself into the saddle. Felicity was already sitting atop Lucy, and she aimed the horses east and north, past the Cowboy Commons, where Dwayne caught sight of three cowboys sitting at the picnic table. Looked like Shane, Austin, and Chadwell—the newest member of the Grape Seed Ranch family.

Dwayne lifted his hand in hello as they passed, and Shane whistled like he'd seen a pretty woman. "You're ridin' that Rocky Mountain horse!" he yelled, as if Dwayne didn't know.

"Don't show off," Felicity muttered and Dwayne glanced at her.

"I'm not showin' off." Though he did feel a bit of pride snaking through him at being able to ride this horse. He'd thought Payday would give him a biggest run for his money, but the horse had succumbed to Dwayne's will pretty readily.

"Mm hm." Felicity gave him a playful smile and urged Lucy into a lope. "Come on. I want to show you something."

"On my own ranch?" He wasn't sure he could get Payday to do much more than walk, and even if he could, it wouldn't be an easy canter that would be comfortable.

"I was riding Linus last week and we found a peach orchard. I wasn't sure if you knew about it."

"Yeah, it's why there's peaches carved into the ranch sign."

"They were wild."

"They're too far away to take care of properly. My mother claimed that she tried, once, when she and my dad first bought the ranch."

"There's a cabin in the midst of them." She looked at him for confirmation, one eyebrow cocked as if to say *Did you know about that?*

"Yeah, sometimes we sleep there when we're out working on those far fences."

She slowed her horse. "Okay, so I can't surprise you. Maybe you could surprise me with something I haven't seen on the ranch."

CHAPTER NINETEEN

Dwayne guided Felicity along a path he'd taken many times. Well, at least when he was growing up, and when he'd finally been discharged from the hospital in Virginia. He hadn't been out to the wishing well for a few years now.

Probably since Serenity left, he thought. He'd made regular trips to the well, tossed in pennies, and asked God to let him know if Serenity was the one for him.

He'd never felt anything one way or the other, and he'd assumed the Lord didn't have time to worry about Dwayne's love life. Now, though, Dwayne believed that God did concern Himself with the details of life. Something his mother had told him growing up had really hit home once Dwayne was left with pieces of his heart from here to Austin.

What's important to you is important to God.

Dwayne did believe that now, though he'd never really seen it at play in his life. "See those trees up there?" He nodded toward the horizon, where the sun shimmered on a line of green. Beyond that, the Bright Star Creek ran right through the ranch.

Several minutes later, he took the lead and ducked under trees he sworn hadn't been this big last time he'd been out here. The wishing well finally came into view, and dismay tore through him when he saw the disrepair it had fallen into.

He dismounted with, "So this here is a wishing well." He dug in his back pocket and took out his thin wallet. "I usually have a coin or two in here." Sure enough, he found a single penny in the corner of the billfold.

"Do you want to do the honors?" He extended the copper coin toward her.

Felicity's face shone with hope, with a radiant light he'd seen a few times—and loved. She didn't immediately reach for the penny, but leaned her weight into the top ring of rocks that made up the well.

"My father and I built this," he said. "When I was about ten. My mother was ill, and Dad needed to get us kids out of the house. He set Heather to raking the leaves and twigs away, and he set me and Thatcher—my brother who lives in Austin? Remember I've mentioned him?"

He glanced at her, and she nodded, that soft smile still sitting on her lips.

"Anyway, Thatcher and I set the stones in place, and cemented them to make the well. Dad had already done the plumbing." Dwayne leaned over the edge of the well and caught the sparkle of sunlight on the water's surface. "After that, we'd come out here whenever we wanted to...I don't know." He exhaled heavily. "When Heather wanted to make the Girl's Choir League, she came out and threw in entire handfuls of her spare change." He chuckled at the memory.

"Right before Thatcher broke the news that he didn't want the ranch, or to stay and work at the ranch, and basically nothing to do with ranching, he camped out here for a solid week."

Dwayne didn't want to tell her about the times he'd made the trips out to the creek and the well. The story spilled from his lips anyway, and when he finished, Felicity had snuggled into his side, her cowgirl hat resting on the well.

"I know this is going to sound bad," she said. "But I'm glad you didn't marry Serenity."

A quick whip of pain hit his heart, and then it beat regularly again. "I am too, Felicity." He pressed his lips to her temple.

She leaned into his touch, kissed the penny, and tossed it into the well without a word. The *plink!* of the coin disappearing into the water met his ears, and Dwayne felt more content than he had in a long, long time. Maybe ever.

If there could be a more perfect morning, Dwayne didn't want to know about it.

———

BY THE END OF SEPTEMBER, FELICITY HAD MORE FRIENDS, MORE fun, and more roots in Grape Seed Falls than she had in Marysville. She'd been in town for three and a half months, and she took a moment each morning to thank the Lord for guiding her here.

The first Sunday in October found her in the backyard, a watering can in her hand. She'd placed potted plants on the patio there, and they were flourishing under her care. Whiskers mewed for breakfast, and she fed him before slipping into the brand new orange dress she'd bought at a boutique in town the day before.

She knotted the leather belt around her waist and put on brown leather cowgirl boots. Though the heat still hovered near summer temperatures, she always marked the arrival of October with new boots. If she acted like it was autumn, maybe Mother Nature would cooperate.

She slid onto the bench next to Dwayne and gave him a quick kiss on the cheek before facing the front. The choir stood in their rows, the bright blue robes swaying as they sang and clapped.

When they finished, Pastor Gifford stood behind the mic and said, "Brothers and Sisters, have you felt God's personal presence in your life?" He leaned forward, something Felicity had seen him do on several occasions when he was trying to make a point. "I know He is there for you. For me. For everyone. Sometimes we might feel abandoned, left alone to weather a storm we think will drown us." His dark eyes swept the congregation. "But if you think that, you're wrong."

His face burst into a wide smile, and Felicity had also heard him say hard things and then soften them with his charm and winning smile.

"God is in the details," Pastor Gifford said. "And I invite you to search those most trying times of your lives—and some of you are living them right now—and see if you can't find Him."

Felicity didn't want to go back to last fall. The anniversary of her father's death was in twenty-three days, and she honestly didn't know how she was going to make it through the hours without a complete breakdown.

Dwayne's fingers on her shoulder tightened, and he removed his arm from around her and took her hand in his.

With him, she thought. She could survive the no-good day if she had Dwayne at her side.

After church ended, Dwayne followed her back to her house, where she'd promised him a lunch of the best fried chicken she could make. He didn't come to her house much, but he fit just fine on the couch, and though he hadn't quite known how to pet Whiskers, he figured it out while she brought oil up to the right temperature and breaded chicken pieces.

"So I got all the stuff you requested for the barbeque sauce," she said when she dropped the first pieces into the pan.

"Oh, right." He leapt from the couch and joined her in the kitchen. They worked together, perfecting a dance in the small space. Felicity liked having him so close, liked the ease with which he measured ingredients and heated them on the stove. She enjoyed the scent of him, and the simple presence of him. She imagined this cooking session to be her permanent reality, and her heart pumped out two extra beats.

His sauce finished at the same time she placed the chicken on paper towels to drain. She pulled the potato salad she'd made the previous afternoon from the fridge and declared lunch served.

Felicity watched as Dwayne bit into her chicken, the crispiness of it crackling through the kitchen. He moaned and his eyes rolled back in his head. He dipped his next bite in his barbeque sauce, and grinned at her. He swallowed. "Really good, Felicity."

He'd said that he was falling in love with her, and she'd said nothing. She wanted to tell him now, that she thought she was definitely falling. Falling as if she'd jumped out of an airplane.

"Dwayne," she said, bringing his attention to her. "I—well, I wanted you to know I think we're good together." She waved her fork toward the kitchen where they'd just worked. "I...liked that." She ducked her head, having never said anything like this to anyone before.

Dwayne's fork clicked against the tabletop as he put it down. "I think we're good together too," he said, his voice thick and low and filled with emotion.

She nodded, warmth spreading through her. They shared a smile that felt a little different to Felicity. Different, how, she wasn't sure. More charged.

More love. The thought entered her mind unbidden, and she basked in the glow of what loving Dwayne might feel like.

Her phone rang, and she jumped up to get it. "It's my brother," she said to Dwayne before saying, "Hey, Gordo. What's goin' on?"

"Felicity...." His voice trailed off, and it wasn't because the line wasn't connected. A muffled sob sounded in her ears, and Felicity spun back to Dwayne. He seemed to scent her panic on the air, because he stood and came toward her.

"Mom's really sick," Gordon finally said. "I think you should come home and see her."

What that meant was *come home and see her before she dies.*

And while Felicity hadn't gotten along very well with her mother, the thought of not having a parent on Earth with her anymore was too much to bear. "I'm coming." She handed the phone to Dwayne and headed down the hall to start packing.

Behind her, his bass voice said words. She pulled out a duffle she'd used on overnight trips out to the far reaches of her family's ranch, but the tears in her eyes made seeing impossible. She collapsed onto the bed and tipped her head back.

"Please," she whispered toward the ceiling, hoping the heartfelt plea would reach all the way to heaven. "Please spare her."

But as Felicity's tears traced hot paths down her cheeks, she knew that even if God didn't spare her mother, He still loved her.

"Hey, hey, hey." Dwayne entered her bedroom and joined her on the bed, pulling her into his chest for safekeeping. "I'll drive you."

She shook her head and sniffled. "No, you can't leave the ranch. I don't even know when I'll be back."

"I'm worried about you making the trip alone."

"I need you to take care of Linus and Lucy for me," she said as if he hadn't expressed concern over anything.

"Of course." He was so strong, so supportive. She felt like they'd become a good team on the ranch, and she prayed with everything she had that God would let her come back to Grape Seed Falls, back to Dwayne.

"And Whiskers," he said. "I'll take 'im out to Chadwell. He has two cats already."

Felicity had only met Chadwell a couple of times, but he seemed capable of keeping a cat alive.

"So." Dwayne stood and drew in a big breath of air. "Let's get you packed. And I want you to call me when you hit the highway, and when you get to Marysville."

Felicity got to her feet and tried to focus, tried to find her jeans and her T-shirts. She wasn't sure what she put in her bag before Dwayne took it to her car.

She turned to face him and he stroked his big hands down the side of her face. "I love you," he said. "Please, please drive carefully." He bent down and kissed her so sweetly, Felicity's eyes teared up again.

It wasn't until she was seated behind the wheel and driving away from him that she whispered, "I love you, too."

CHAPTER TWENTY

"I made it," Felicity said into her phone, the words appearing on the screen so she could text them to Dwayne. She stared at the house, wondering what lay hidden behind that front door her father had hung himself.

She hadn't dared utter another prayer. She didn't want to do the same things she'd done the last time she was in crisis. She wanted to have more faith than last time. More power over what she chose to do.

After sending the message, she steeled herself and got out of the car. She could handle whatever sat behind the door. She could.

Parker exited before she could climb the steps. "Felicity." He gave her a quick hug.

"Just tell me." Felicity hugged herself and couldn't quite meet her brother's eyes.

"No one knows. But she just keeps getting worse and worse."

"There's no diagnosis?"

Parker shook her head and sighed as he leaned against the porch railing. "All of her blood work came back normal. She doesn't have an infection that they can find. But she's tired all the time, and she's got a cough she can't shake."

The door creaked and Gordon came outside. He embraced Felicity and stuck his hands in his pockets. She hadn't spent a lot of time with him over the past several months, but she'd seen this tactic before.

"What is it?" she asked.

"Mom has been diagnosed."

"What?" Parker said at the same time as Felicity.

"I wanted to tell you together." He removed his hat and ran his hand through his hair. "It's thyroid cancer."

Cancer echoed in Felicity's head.

"When did you find out?"

"Friday afternoon."

"Two days?" Parker was almost shouting. "You didn't tell me for two days?"

"I wanted Felicity to be here."

"You didn't even call her until an hour ago." Parker's anger stained the very air around them.

"Cancer," Felicity said, hoping to diffuse the situation. "How bad is it?"

"They aren't sure," Gordon exhaled, the sound full of defeat. "The oncologist wants to remove the entire thyroid, and then he'll know more."

"When will that happen?" Felicity asked.

"Three weeks." Gordon nodded toward the door. "C'mon. I told her you were here, so she's probably trying to get out of bed right now."

Mom lay in bed, the TV on the dresser flickering in front of her. "Mom." Felicity drank in the gray color of her face, the absolute exhaustion on her face. The curtains had been drawn completely closed, leaving the room mostly dark except for the light from the television.

"Felicity." Her mother didn't try to smile, but she did lift her hand. Felicity took it between both of hers. "What are you doing here?"

"Gordon said you were sick." The room itself smelled like

death. "I came to see you." She glanced up and met her oldest brother's eyes. The hope there made Felicity's heart crash against her ribcage "I'm going to...stay for a while to help you...around here."

She saw the resigned look in Gordon's eyes, and she couldn't help the crack that started somewhere in her new cowgirl boots and finished right in the middle of her heart.

A week later, she arrived back in Grape Seed Falls, without makeup and without the opportunity to stay for more than a couple of hours. She packed a much bigger suitcase this time and stopped by Capri's, though her friend was at work. She'd promised to take care of the yard and go out to the ranch and explain everything to Dwayne.

Felicity couldn't bear to do it. If she allowed herself to see him again, she wouldn't be able to leave him or the ranch. And her mother needed her. It wouldn't be forever, and she'd have to hope that there would still be a spot open in Dwayne's heart for her when she could return.

He wasn't supposed to be in town this weekend anyway, as the auction in Austin was in full swing. She still couldn't chance going out to the ranch, not even to see Linus and Lucy. She'd call Levi when he returned from the auction and arrange for him to go get her horses and board them.

She hoped the fact that she hadn't given up her lease, that she was leaving her horses here, would alert Dwayne to the fact that she would be returning to Grape Seed Falls. Returning to him.

I love you. His words echoed in her mind for the entire drive back to Marysville.

———

DWAYNE CLIMBED INTO THE CAB OF HIS TRUCK AFTER SECURING Levi's trailer to the hitch. "You ready for this?"

"I've got my eye on a horse or two." Levi rolled down the

window and rested his elbow on the doorframe. "What about you?"

"Maybe more than one or two," Dwayne said, his tone a bit darker than he intended. He'd been missing Felicity like crazy, as she hadn't answered either of his phone calls that week and had only sent him short sentences about what was going on with her mother.

He was trying not to worry, trying not to stress, trying not to give in to the urge to swing by Marysville on his way to Austin. He'd talked to Heather this week, and she'd advised him to lay low, give Felicity some time to absorb the bad health news, and let her call when she was ready.

If only it didn't make him want to abandon everything he'd built over the past fifteen years of working on the ranch. He couldn't stand the thought of her alone on the ranch, or worse, alone with her mother.

She's not alone, he told himself for the twelfth time. Her brothers were there. But she didn't have her horses or her cat, and Dwayne's heart stuttered in its beat.

Heather had also expressly forbidden him to talk to Levi about Capri, or dating, or women at all. But Dwayne was desperate for something to talk about. So he said, "So, whatever happened with you and Capri?"

"Capri?"

"Yeah, that blonde woman who lives next door to Felicity?" Dwayne glanced at Levi, who seemed genuinely perplexed. "She's a mechanic?"

"Oh, right. The mechanic."

"You seriously don't remember her?"

"We went out a coupla times," Levi said. "She's nice, but...." He shrugged. "I don't know. There wasn't a spark."

Dwayne would've normally left the conversation at that. Heck, he normally would have never started a conversation like this one. But the word vomit was coming up and he was going to have to ask.

"So what does cause a spark for you?"

Thankfully, Levi didn't seem to know Dwayne was probing on behalf of his sister. "I don't know," he said. "I guess I like blondes. I don't know. There's just no one in town that's interesting."

"Where are you lookin'?"

"Oh, I'm not lookin'." He waved his hand like such a notion was ridiculous. "The horses keep me too busy, and running a ranch is a lot different than just workin' on one."

"You're not kidding." Dwayne had weathered that as well, and he ended his line of questioning. He glanced down the road that would take him to Marysville as he passed, his knuckles tightening on the steering wheel.

"How are you and Felicity?"

"Just fine." Dwayne thought about the last words he'd spoken out loud to her. *I love you.* She looked like she was ready to say it back to him too, but she hadn't. He shouldn't have put it on her when she'd just found out about her mother.

Didn't matter. He'd seen the love in her eyes. Felt it in her touch. So she hadn't said it in so many words. Didn't matter. He knew.

They arrived at the horse auction, and the bay horse that Dwayne had kept his eye on all these weeks stood in the stall on the end, almost taunting him to come over and say hello. Dwayne wanted the horse the moment he approached and the animal lifted its head over the top rung, as if it sensed in Dwayne a kindred spirit.

"Hey, there," he said, rubbing both hands up the horse's neck and looking into his eyes. He didn't stay too long, mostly because he didn't want anyone else to see him showing so much interest in the bay. Starting prices and up-bidders would make him pay a hefty price if he did that. After all, this auction wasn't his first. He feigned interest in the other horses, but he really just wanted the bay.

The auction started, and Dwayne handed over his ticket and found a seat next to Levi. "Did you see anything interesting?"

"Yeah."

"Which one?"

"Number eight."

Dwayne's throat went dry. "*I* want number eight." He didn't even have to look at the lineup.

"The bay?"

"Yeah, the bay." Dwayne wondered how much money Levi had brought with him, and if he'd really have to get into a bidding war with the man.

Levi consulted the lineup. "I like the Arabian too," he said.

"Yeah," Dwayne said noncommittally. He didn't want the Arabian. He wanted the bay, and he'd bought a lot of cash to make it happen.

When it was time for the bay, he put in the first bid.

"Oh, so you're serious." Levi grinned at him.

"It's the only horse I want." Dwayne didn't look away from the auctioneer—or the man in the third row who'd just outbid him. Dwayne let a few seconds go by as he scanned the crowd, as the auctioneer spoke so fast, his lips were a blur.

Finally, he put in another bid. The man in row three turned, but Dwayne had already put his hand down. A back-and-forth war began, and with five exchanges under his belt, Dwayne finally won the bay.

Relief poured through him, and he smiled for all he was worth. Levi congratulated him, but really Dwayne wished Felicity sat next to him. He wondered what she'd be like in an auction situation. Cool, calm, collected? Or nervous and admonishing him not to spend too much?

Didn't matter. He wanted her by his side at an auction. At his house. On the ranch. On the pew at church. Everywhere.

He needed to call her again, and he promised himself he would tomorrow before church.

When he finally got back to the ranch, and got the bay all settled in a box stall, he found Capri of all people sitting on his front steps.

"Capri?" he asked as he approached. Alarms sounded in his soul, but he couldn't run away now. "What are you doin' here?"

She stood, and while Dwayne didn't know her well, he'd interacted with her several times, usually after church as he and Felicity were leaving.

"Felicity wanted me to come out and talk to you," she said. She shoved her hands in a dirty pair of shorts she'd obviously spent the day wearing while she repaired cars.

Dwayne didn't know what to say. "You wanna come in?" he asked.

She shook her head. "No, thanks. She said to let you know that she's going to call Levi and arrange for Linus and Lucy to be boarded there."

"She doesn't need to do that." He'd enjoyed feeding her horses and letting them out to pasture. It was the only link he had to her, as Whiskers had disappeared inside Chadwell's house, never to be seen again.

Capri shrugged. "You can tell her that, I guess." She looked uncomfortable and proved it by shifting her feet left and then right. "She told me to let you know that she hasn't given up her lease, and she's boarding her horses in town, but she doesn't know when she'll be back."

Dwayne's chest turned cold. "She doesn't?"

"She has to quit out here at Grape Seed Ranch. Dwayne, I'm so sorry."

He didn't care about having Felicity here as his horse trainer. He wanted her here as his wife. "I'll call her."

"Her mother has thyroid cancer, and they're working out all the treatment possibilities," Capri said quickly. "She's real busy, and... well, she probably won't answer."

He blinked at the other woman, realization after realization crashing on top of him, crushing him. "She's breaking up with me, isn't she?"

"Her note didn't say that," Capri said. "She just doesn't know when she'll be able to come back. She said she'd understand if you didn't want to wait."

Didn't want to wait.

Didn't want to wait? Why wouldn't he wait? He was in love with the woman, for crying out loud.

"Sorry, Dwayne." Capri started to back away, and Dwayne watched her go, unsure as to what had just happened.

He pulled out his phone and dialed Felicity, begging God with everything he had that she would pick up.

"Please pick up," he whispered. "Please pick up."

CHAPTER TWENTY-ONE

Felicity didn't pick up his call. Or the next one he placed after he'd showered. Or the one he dialed before bed. Sunday morning found him on the bay's back, contemplating a name for his new horse and guiding the animal toward the wishing well.

This was a good horse, who'd done everything Dwayne had asked of it the first time. "I think I'll name you King," he told the horse, his words almost getting swept away in the fall wind that had picked up.

At the wishing well, Dwayne just stared into its depths while King snacked on the long grasses nearby. He hadn't brought any coins, knew wishing wouldn't bring Felicity back.

She kept her cottage, he thought. *Her horses are here.*

"She's coming back," he whispered, the words feeling right and comforting in his throat. But why wouldn't she talk to him? Why had she sent her neighbor out to tell him?

Something had changed in the week she'd been gone, but Dwayne didn't know what.

Determined to drive all the way to Marysville if he had to,

Dwayne swung onto King's back and urged him toward the homestead.

Before he had a signal on his cell, and before he'd returned to the barn, a horse appeared on the horizon. Dwayne had told exactly one person where he was going that morning. Sure enough, Kurt appeared, breathless and with panic written all over his face.

"What is it?" Dwayne asked, his nerves firing on all cylinders. If Tiger had broken the fence again, Dwayne didn't know what he'd do.

Kurt swung his horse around and came alongside Dwayne. "Your dad," the foreman wheezed. "Collapsed and we can't wake him up."

FELICITY VOLUNTEERED TO STAY HOME WITH MOMMA WHILE her brothers went to church. She hoped Dwayne would call again, and she could sneak out to the back porch and answer his call. He didn't call, and Momma woke up with such a fit of coughing that blood came up.

Felicity had a very bad feeling that her mother's condition was a lot more than thyroid cancer. She slept a lot, leaving Felicity to the household chores, the grocery shopping, the meal preparation. As the days passed, her mood worsened and worsened—especially because Dwayne had stopped calling altogether.

"You have a phone," she muttered to herself. "You know his number." And yet, she couldn't get herself to dial it. Instead, she mopped, she washed sheets, she fed her brothers, and herself, and had to force-feed Momma. She rarely went outside anymore, and the bluebonnets on the ranch sign still hadn't been stained.

By the weekend, Felicity was starting to feel like she'd never escape the walls of the house, get away from her mother, or be herself ever again. She lay in bed early on Saturday morning, her thoughts far from her father, far from the bluebonnets, far from everything except one person.

Dwayne.

She thought about cooking with him that last time. Riding out to the wishing well. Having a family with him.

Bolting to a sitting position, her heart started hammering. Once she had children, would she be as confined to the house as she felt now, taking care of her mother?

Hot tears pricked her eyes. If so, she couldn't do that. Her spirit longed to be free, riding horses with the wind pulling at her cowgirl hat. She had liked fixing fences, and facing down bulls, and she'd wished with all her heart she could've gone to the horse auction with Dwayne.

Nowhere in there had she considered what having a family would do to her ability to leave walls behind and experience the Texas ranch she'd grown to love.

She and Dwayne hadn't specifically talked about having kids, but Felicity assumed he'd want them, want someone to leave the ranch to once he was ready to retire. He'd made it clear Thatcher didn't want it, and Heather taught school in town.

Her heart raced faster when she heard a moan from the bedroom next door. With feet that practically flew, she headed into Momma's room to help her. A sense of suffocation enveloped her, and a sob worked its way up Felicity's throat.

"Let me get you a drink," she managed to say before escaping the room in favor of the kitchen, where Parker stood at the sink, gazing out the window.

"Momma needs a drink," Felicity said, her voice breaking on the last word. She didn't wait to see if Parker would get it for her. She had to get out of this house. Get out now.

HOURS LATER, SHE CLIMBED THE STEPS OF THE FIRE TRUCK, THE way she'd done for years. Uncle Ezra had responded to her desperate call immediately, and her soul quieted with each stair she put behind her. She wanted to keep going; climb all the way through the atmosphere and right into the heavens. Anything not to have to return to the house.

She hadn't been back inside except to change out of her pajamas and into her more comfortable jeans and T-shirt, and she'd texted her brothers that she would do the morning feeding if they would please help with Momma today.

"You okay?" Uncle Ezra called up the ladder, and Felicity gave him a thumbs up. She carefully reached into her back pocket and took out the paintbrush Daddy had been using on these bluebonnets for decades.

She set the jar of pennies and vinegar she'd carried up with her on the top rung of the ladder and twisted off the lid. The acidic scent had made her wince the first time, and her father had chuckled at her. Now the vinegary smell made her chest tighten with loss. Steadfastly, and with determination, she dipped the brush into the homemade blue stain, and swirled it around to really get the darkest bluebonnet blue she could get.

As she worked, everything that had grown tight inside her loosened. This was what Felicity was meant to do with her life. Not laundry, and vacuuming, and making peanut butter and jelly sandwiches. Ranch work, and horse training, and afternoons out on the open range.

How she'd never known that she didn't want children upset her. Frustration made the brush slip a little, and paint part of the stem the wrong color. Felicity drew in a deep breath and steadied herself.

She hadn't known, because Dwayne was the first man ever to make her think long-term. Make her think outside the ranch. Make her consider being a wife.

"I want that," she muttered to the pesky top of a bluebonnet that wouldn't seem to accept the stain. She went back to the jar again and again, and still the color wouldn't stick. Like lightning, she realized she'd been doing the same thing. Going to church over and over, the message never really sticking in her mind.

She finally got the bluebonnet the right color. "There you go, Daddy," she whispered before capping the vinegar bottle and heading down the steps. Uncle Ezra lowered the ladder and gave her a side-hug.

"He loved those bluebonnets," he said.

"He sure did." Felicity turned back to the house to find her brothers and Momma sitting on the porch. Resignation made her shoulders droop. "You want to come in for lunch, Uncle Ezra? I'm sure I can whip something up."

"If you're half as good of a cook as your momma, I'm sure you can."

Felicity pressed her lips together. She wasn't half as good as her mom, she knew that. But she knew how to put butter and cheese on bread and toast it up fine.

"Thank you, Felicity," Gordon said as she passed him, and confusion pulled through her. She wasn't sure what he needed to thank her for. Coming home and caring for their mother? Painting the bluebonnets? Simply being there?

Felicity frowned as a surge of fury reared through her like a tsunami. He hadn't given up a single thing to have her there, or to look after Momma, or to keep working on the ranch. But Felicity felt like she'd lost everything that mattered to her.

She made it through lunch by talking to Uncle Ezra about the little petting zoo he ran now that he was retired. He could talk about goats and ponies forever, and she let him, hoping she'd be able to face the afternoon once he left.

After waving good-bye to him from the driveway, Felicity tucked both hands in her back pockets, her confusion and anger still swirling through her. Dodging, lifting, twisting the way hot and cold air currents did when they made a cyclone.

Without talking to or texting anyone, she got in her car and went to the only place she could think of to find peace and clarity. She went to the little red-brick church she'd grown up attending. But she didn't go inside the chapel. She didn't need more walls.

The cemetery stretched along the west and north side of the church, and her feet took her that way. She paused at the gate, hesitant to walk down this memory lane. She hadn't been to her father's final resting place once, the emotions too fresh and too raw.

But as she made her way across the grass, the breeze the only sound in the warm afternoon, the sense of sorrow and foreboding left her. Peace replaced it, and by the time she gazed down at her father's headstone, Felicity knew why she'd come.

"Daddy." She bent and traced her fingertips across the top of the stone. "I met the most wonderful man." Tears splashed the dark gray rock, and Felicity sat next to her father's gravesite and looked out across the horizon.

"This is a great place to be buried," she told him. "I'm sure you like the view. You can almost see the ranch from here." She fell silent for a while after that, her thoughts moving slowly, as if they'd been caught in cooling tar. She finally started talking about Dwayne again, and how she'd fallen in love with him, and how she thought sure she'd lose him once she confessed she didn't want children.

Her father never answered, but Felicity could *feel* him nearby. She wondered how she'd left Marysville, and if perhaps she'd made a mistake in moving to Grape Seed Falls. Her bewilderment and frustration returned, because she'd felt whole and at peace there too. She'd made friends, and been happy, and fallen in love.

So where should she be?

She leaned back on her hands and stretched her legs out in front of her, tipping her face toward the sun.

"Where should I be?" she asked the Lord, hoping with everything in her that He would respond in a way that made sense to her. Several seconds of silence passed, and Felicity felt nothing inside. Only the beating of her heart, which seemed to slow the way it did when she fell asleep.

Then she heard, "There you are," in a voice she swore she

knew. A voice that belonged to her heart. A voice that tickled her eardrums, that she'd daydreamed about waking up next to, that never got angry or lifted in frustration.

Her eyes shot open, but she couldn't focus because of the bright sun. "Dwayne?"

CHAPTER TWENTY-TWO

"Just me." Gordon approached slowly, casting Felicity in shadow before dropping to the ground beside her. "Sorry."

She told her heart to settle down, that Dwayne was far away, probably interviewing a new horse trainer already. She wondered if he'd purchased the bay at the auction, and if so, what he'd named the horse.

"So you really like this guy."

Felicity wanted to deny it, but her voice wouldn't betray her heart. "Yeah." She sighed. "I really like him."

"Maybe you should go visit him this weekend. We'll be okay with Momma."

Felicity's chin trembled as she tried to hold back the tears. "I don't think he'll want to talk to me."

"No? Why not?"

She sniffled and waved her hand at nothing. "I haven't answered any of his calls, and he stopped trying earlier this week."

Gordon sat on the information for several long seconds. "Why didn't you answer?"

What a great question. Who had she been trying to spare? Dwayne? Herself? From what, exactly?

"He's a busy man," she finally said. "He owns and operates the ranch."

"He doesn't have a foreman?"

"He does."

"Then he can take a phone call. Or a weekend to see you. Or whatever else he wants."

Felicity didn't like how Gordon was making it sound it was Dwayne who'd done something wrong. Instead of defending him, she asked, "What should I do?"

"Well, it's clear you're miserable here," Gordon said. "Parker and I hate that we've asked you to come when you have something you'd rather do somewhere else."

"It's not that I'd rather be somewhere else." But it was. Sort of. "I just...I wasn't made to clean bathrooms, make dinner, and sit in the house."

"I know."

"I want to be here and help. But I—I can't stay in the house all the time." She met her brother's eye with desperation and panic in hers. "I just can't. Maybe we could work out a rotation."

"We will." He stood and brushed the leaves off his jeans. "First thing Monday."

"Monday?" Felicity scrambled to her feet too. Maybe she could go to church early tomorrow, stay late....

"Yeah." Gordon swung a wicked smile at her. "You're going home for the weekend."

"I am home," she said.

"No, you're not." He walked away, leaving her to wonder when he had become so astute about matters of the heart. She watched him go, torn between jumping in her car and heading to Grape Seed Falls immediately, or hurrying home to make dinner for Momma.

God, it seemed, did not have an opinion either way.

THE FOLLOWING MORNING, FELICITY DID INDEED LEAVE THE house early for church. Gordon had speared her with a daggered gaze when she'd returned last night. She hadn't offered any explanations. She didn't have any.

Dwayne had told her that his favorite part of his Sabbath Day worship was listening to the music. He claimed to arrive at church fifteen minutes early just to listen to the organist, or maybe catch the tail end of the choir as they practiced.

Felicity, on the other hand, always showed up a few minutes late, as if that way no one would see her attending the meeting. She wasn't embarrassed about going to church—it seemed everyone in these small Texas towns did—but she didn't want anyone to know she didn't really belong there.

But not today. Oh no. Today, she got to the red brick church early, parked in the front row, and entered the building to the magnificence of the organ. Voices filled the rafters moments later, and she had arrived before the choir had finished their rehearsal.

She paused, took a deep breath, and ducked into the back row of the chapel. Two white-haired ladies sat right up front—the Butler sisters. Both widowed, they'd moved in together a few years ago. Felicity had gone with her father to help move the bigger items, and a smile touched her lips for a moment with the kind memory.

Closing her eyes, she let the music flow over and around her. Through her. Something stirred inside her. Something she hadn't felt for a long time.

Something that whispered she needed to get to Grape Seed Ranch right now.

Without hesitating, and with a heart about to burst with gratitude for this tiny, microscopic whisper she could barely hear, she leapt from the bench and ran back to her car.

DWAYNE WASN'T TAKING ANY CALLS EXCEPT THOSE FROM KURT

and Heather. If someone knocked on his door, he didn't answer it. He simply didn't have any more to give.

Guilt riddled him, but Kurt assured him that the ranch was running just fine without him and that he should take as much time as he needed to be with his family.

The doctors had found one of his father's arteries to be blocked, which had caused the shortness of breath he'd complained about to Dwayne's mother, the tingling in his right arm he hadn't mentioned to anyone until questioned by the heart surgeon, and the eventual unconsciousness.

With rest and strict orders to pay attention to how he felt, he'd been discharged from the hospital a week ago now that it was the Sabbath again. He'd stayed down too, and Dwayne usually spent the mornings with him so his mother could get things done in the yard and around the house.

He had a surgery scheduled to put a stent in the artery to keep it open in a couple of weeks. Until then, Dwayne didn't want him to be alone.

In the afternoons, Dwayne worked with Spotlight. The horse was almost completely trained now, and he wanted the animal to be ready whenever Felicity returned. But with each passing day, he wondered if she even would. To torture himself further, he'd started stalking the FOR RENT section of the Grape Seed Falls online classifieds. If her house went up for rent, he'd know she wasn't coming back.

He had to do *something*.

She hadn't returned a single call or text of his in almost two weeks, and the last three words he'd said to her had turned pointed and sharp. They stabbed into his lungs every time he thought about telling her he loved her.

This pain was much, much worse than when Serenity had broken their engagement. Dwayne knew now what true love felt like, and that was why he couldn't see anyone, talk to anyone. His existence was okay if he limited himself to his family and Kurt.

He'd been planning to skip church completely, skip all interaction for the day. But Heather had texted *Mom's making ghost pancakes*, and that had changed Dwayne's mind in a heartbeat.

When he was growing up, his mother made pancakes for breakfast every Sunday morning. She colored the batter for holidays, and used cookie cutters to make special characters. And ghost pancakes meant buttermilk batter with chocolate chip eyes. For some reason, Dwayne loved them. Because he'd loved growing up on the ranch. Loved growing up in his family, with his parents, with Thatcher and Heather.

The desire to have a family of his own like the one he'd had made his throat so narrow he could barely swallow.

Someone knocked on his door, and he stepped away from it.

"I know you're in there," Heather called. She tried the doorknob, but it just clicked back and forth. "C'mon, Dwayne. Come eat breakfast with us."

He strode to the door and opened it. Sunlight streamed in, reminding him of how much he loved being outdoors. "I'm comin'."

She scanned him from head to toe. "Not going to church, I see."

"I already told you I wasn't." He stepped out onto the porch. "Leave me be."

She joined him as he went down the steps. "Oh, come on. She's going to come back."

"You don't know that," he practically growled.

"Want me to go talk to her?"

"No."

"Well, I might just do it anyway, the way you talked to Levi when I told you not to."

Dwayne stalled, his feet growing roots right there in the grass. "How did you find out?" He hadn't said anything to her. He'd barely been home from the auction when his father had fallen.

A hint of redness entered her face. "He talked to me on Friday. First time in months." Heather looked down and twisted a lock of her hair around and around. "He asked how much you liked Felicity, because he hated seeing you like this, and he was hoping to set you up with someone."

Dwayne didn't know what to say. He only breathed and blinked because his body did it involuntarily.

"Eventually, it came out that you'd asked him what kind of women he liked." She tossed her hair over her shoulder. "At least I'm already blonde."

Her grin unstopped his vocal chords, and he laughed for the first time in days. After he sobered, he said, "I didn't mention you, I swear."

"I know you didn't."

"He's a real idiot for not seein' you there, right in front of him."

She smiled but it wobbled a little. "I keep telling myself that too." She linked her arm through his, and they started much slower toward the homestead. "But come on. You really don't think Felicity will come back?"

"I honestly don't know."

"So how much of your sequestering has to do with her, and how much with Dad?"

He sighed, avoiding a hole in the ground. "All her." He could deal with his father. He had. They had a solution. His dad was going to be fine. But Dwayne seriously doubted that he would ever be whole without Felicity.

The scent of browning pancakes and hot maple syrup met his nose a good ten yards from the back door. At least something in Grape Seed Falls hadn't changed, and Dwayne's spirits lifted the teensiest bit.

"Hey, Mom." He pressed a kiss to his mother's forehead. "Looks great."

Heather said grace, and Dwayne loaded his plate with three ghosts and more sausage links that any human should eat. He poured syrup over all of it and sat down to eat. His father said something, and his mother laughed, and Dwayne basked in the happiness from the two of them. They'd always been so positive, even when things hadn't gone well on the ranch. And they loved each other.

Dwayne bit the head off one of his ghosts, his mood shifting toward the negative again. His own parents were making him jealous. Would he have to stop seeing them too?

Someone rang the doorbell, making everyone pause. "Who could that be?" his mother asked, abandoning her post at the griddle to answer the door. If it was Kurt, he'd have walked in the back door. One of the cowboys would've knocked and then walked in the back door.

No one rang the front doorbell. Dwayne was surprised it actually worked. He didn't care. Whoever it was hadn't come here to see him.

"Dwayne." His mother appeared in the doorway that led into the living room and then the foyer.

He glanced up, his pulse panicking at the shock on his mother's face. "It's for you," she said.

"Who is it?"

"Go see."

"Mom." He stayed put at the dining room table.

"I'll go see." Heather jumped to her feet and threw Dwayne a mischievous smile. She hadn't taken two steps into the other room before her gasp and cry of surprise seemed to happen simultaneously.

"Come see," she said, flapping her hand for him to rush forward.

With both of them conspiring against them, he slowly left his pancakes to see who was at the door. His mind raced with possibilities. He stopped and looked down at Heather. "Just tell me who it is," he begged.

She moved behind him and pushed him through the doorway. "Go. See."

Dwayne also stalled just inside the other room. His eyes

needed a check-up, because the one person he'd wanted to see, to talk to, to hold and comfort for the past two weeks stood in his parents' foyer.

"Felicity."

CHAPTER TWENTY-THREE

Dwayne's legs felt weak and strong at the same time. Thankfully, they moved without express direction from his brain. He had so many things to say to her, and a lot of explanations he needed to hear.

But the very sight of her, standing there with her hands in her pockets, that worried look on her face, rocking back onto her heels and then onto her toes.

He entered her personal space, his hands slipping around her waist and pulling her into an embrace. "Felicity," he repeated, his voice hardly his own. He was aware that his family was watching, and he didn't care. Stepping back, he ran his hands down the sides of her face as if to check and see if she was real. "You came back."

"Hey." She tiptoed her fingertips up his chest, sending shivers through his whole body. "I can't stay, but I really wanted to see you."

"Do you want breakfast? My mom made pancakes."

"Uh...." She glanced past him. "Maybe we could go for a walk. Or ride Linus and Lucy."

Dwayne saw something in her expression, but he couldn't identify it. "Sure." He guided her toward the door while turning back to his family. "We're gonna go ride for a bit. Thanks for the pancakes, Mom."

His stomach quivered as they stepped outside, because he knew the hard conversations were about to start.

As soon as the door closed behind them, Felicity blurted, "I'm really sorry I didn't answer your calls. I was in a bad place, and I didn't want to drag you there too." Her chest heaved with pent-up emotion.

Dwayne hummed as he gathered her close and trailed his lips along her jawline. "Doesn't matter now." He touched his mouth to hers, and while Felicity had had every intention of telling him everything first, she kissed him back.

She pulled away long before she wanted to. "It *does* matter," she said. "My mom is pretty sick, and that was hard on me. I thought for a few days last week that I could come back here, but the more time I spend in Marysville, the more I think I won't be able to."

"Hey, it's okay." He took her hand and led her toward the stable. "Let's take one thing at a time. Your mom. She's really sick?"

"Thyroid cancer she needs surgery for. We've got a date scheduled, but it's still a couple of weeks out."

"Same with my dad."

"Your dad?"

"I mean, not the thyroid cancer, but he has to have a stent put in his artery. He fainted last week, and we found out he has almost one-hundred percent blockage in one of his arteries leading into his heart."

Felicity stopped walking, Dwayne's wonderful voice reverberating inside her skull. "Your dad...he fainted last week?" And she hadn't been here to support Dwayne. Hadn't answered any of his calls. "Is that why you stopped calling?"

He wouldn't look fully at her. "Didn't think you'd notice if I stopped calling." He cleared his throat. "But yeah, I was dealing with a lot, and adding silence from you whenever I called hurt too much."

The wounds in her heart cracked a little more. "I'm so sorry."

"Apology accepted." He tugged on her hand and got her going toward the stable again.

He moved steadily down the aisle to where Linus and Lucy were housed, but Felicity noticed the new horse in the end stall. "Oh, what have we here?" She turned to Dwayne and cocked one eyebrow. "Looks like you got the bay."

Joy exploded through her. He'd wanted that horse, and she was glad he'd gotten him.

"It wasn't easy," Dwayne said, stepping over to the handsome horse. "I probably paid way too much for him. But we've ridden several times, and he's a great horse." He glanced at her. "Already broken."

"What'd you name him?"

"King."

The horse held a royal air about him, so Felicity said, "Seems like it fits him well."

Dwayne gave King one last scratch and went down the aisle. They worked to saddle the horses in silence, and when Felicity boosted herself onto Lucy's back, the stars seemed to align.

"I painted the bluebonnets," she said.

"On the ranch sign? That's great."

"My brothers and I are working out a schedule to take care of my mom."

He nodded and nudged Linus forward. "When do you think...?"

"I don't know, Dwayne. I don't even really know what I'm doing here. I just know I went to church early to listen to the music, and I felt like I should come."

Lucy stepped, stepped, stepped before Dwayne said, "You went to church early to listen to the music?"

"Yeah." She shrugged one shoulder. "You said you liked it, and I thought I'd give it a try."

"So you came to tell me...." He let the statement hang there, and Felicity had no idea how to fill it.

"I wanted to apologize," she said.

"You've done that."

"And...I don't know. I just felt like I should come." She had something else to discuss with him, but she couldn't bring herself to bring up the subject of having kids. His mother had just made pancakes for the family, and all of her children were well into their adult years.

"But you don't know if you can come back to Grape Seed Ranch."

"I don't know that, no."

He gazed out at the horizon, the wheels in his mind obviously churning. She gave him the time he needed to organize everything, because she needed it too.

"Do you love me?" he finally asked, his voice barely louder than the hoofbeats on the ground.

"Yes," she whispered without any hesitation.

"All right. Then I can wait for however long it takes for you to come back."

She loved the way he drawled out *allll riiight*. She thought about the first time she'd heard him say that, and a smile graced her face. It didn't last long, though, as her brain seemed to constantly remind her of what needed to be said.

"I have something I want to talk to you about," she said. "Something I've realized while I've been home these past two weeks."

"Something we haven't talked about already?"

"Yes, something we haven't discussed yet." She suddenly found her mouth void of saliva. "A family," she forced out. "Kids. I—I—I don't want kids." She said the last four words in a huge rush.

Dwayne gaped openly at her now. "You don't? Why not?"

Felicity's heart dropped to her boots and rebounded to the back of her throat. In her fantasies, when she told Dwayne her feelings about children, he said, "It's no problem. I don't want children either."

But it was obvious the opposite was true in her reality.

"I—I'm not cut out to cook and clean and care for children all day." She could turn Lucy around here and find nothing but blue sky, fences, and waving prairie grasses. "I don't want to make pancakes for breakfast, or have dinner waiting on the table when you come in from the ranch. I want to be *out on the ranch*, fixing fences, and repairing equipment, and hauling hay, and training horses."

A dark edge entered his normally sparkling blue eyes. "And you think havin' kids will make it so you can't do those things." He didn't phrase it as a question, but Felicity nodded anyway.

"I've seen what my mother does. It's not the life I want." She didn't realize how much punch her words carried until he visibility flinched.

"It's the only life I have to offer you," he said, his voice full of agony.

"That's not true," she said. "I love you, and you love me, and we could work this ranch together."

"And then what? Sell it?"

Everything she'd worried about, every fear she'd experienced, had been right. And Felicity had never wanted to be wrong about something as much as she did right then.

Dwayne exhaled, his head held slightly away from her so she couldn't read his expression. She disliked this new distance between them, but didn't know how to fix it.

"So you came here to break up with me," he said.

"No." She shook her head. "Not at all."

"I want a family, Felicity," he said, his voice even and deep and beautiful. "A whole house full of them. I want boys to love the ranch and horses as much as I do, and I want daughters to learn to rope and ride the way you do."

And when he said it like that, she wanted those things too.

"I'm wonderin' why you think it has to be one or the other," he said. "I know how to make pancakes, and do laundry, and put shoes on a kid. Well, maybe not that last part, but I'm sure I could figure it out."

She'd never seen her father help around the house. He'd never driven her to school or picked her up. He worked the ranch, plain and simple. Her mother did everything else.

"I guess you're right," Felicity said. "I can work the ranch and be a mom."

"I don't see why not," Dwayne said, finally nudging his horse closer to hers. "It would be a partnership, Felicity. I might be better at laundry than you anyway."

Her eyes flew to his, and she found love and laughter there. "I know I'm better at cookin'."

"You are not."

"Name one thing you can make better than I can."

"Uh, just about everything, Mister. Remember that pasta salad I made for the block party?"

"Did you really just say your pasta salad is better than my family recipe, which has won at three Family Festivals?"

She burst out laughing. "I forgot about the prize-winning salad."

"I don't see how that's even possible."

Her heart soared with love for Dwayne. She'd never said the words, so she let them loose now. "I love you, Dwayne."

He pulled his horse in front of hers and dismounted in one fluid movement. His right hand shook twice as hard as she'd ever seen it when he stepped to her side and took her left hand in his.

"I love you too." He kissed her wrist. "I want you to marry me and be my wife, my partner, my everything on this ranch." He gazed up at her with adoration, hope, and anxiety.

"I want that too." A twinge of fear still stuck in her throat. "I do have to go back to Marysville and help my family, though."

"Of course."

"And I want to make sure I know what you'll do and what I'll do within our family."

"We'll talk about it all and decide everything together."

Felicity grinned down and him and slipped from the saddle and into his arms. "All right then."

"All right then," he said just before matching his mouth to hers for the most wonderful kiss of her life. Because she wouldn't have to be trapped inside the homestead when she wanted to be free in the wilderness. Because she loved Dwayne Carver and had told him. Because she'd listened to the Lord when He prompted her to come back here and make things right.

CHAPTER TWENTY-FOUR

Felicity found she could endure more household tasks and curb her cravings to work outside after her reconciliation with Dwayne. If she was frustrated about something, she called him. She told him about how she and Gordon had agreed that she'd only make dinner on Mondays, Wednesdays, and Sundays, but then he acted put out where there wasn't anything to eat on Friday.

He'd ordered pizza—problem solved. "And not my problem," she'd ranted to Dwayne, who'd taken it all and offered nothing but support in return.

Her mother's thyroid came out in mid-November, and she started to feel a bit better after that. The medication she'd have to take for the rest of her life actually provided what her thyroid should've been giving her all this time, so there was definitely some improvement.

Felicity began to feel like every day was another day closer to when she could return to Grape Seed Falls, return to Dwayne.

When her mother's blood work all came back within the right range for the next step of the treatment—swallowing a radiation pill—she called Dwayne again.

"Hey, there," he answered easily. "I just finished brushing down Lucy."

"Oh yeah? How is she?" A pang of homesickness hit Felicity, which didn't make a lot of sense to her. But maybe Gordon had been right. This ranch wasn't her home anymore. Her heart had left it the day her father died.

"Doin' great. I think you might have to convince her you own her when you get back." He chuckled. "Chadwell's taken a liking to her, and she follows him all over the ranch on the weekends."

"You tell Chadwell he can get himself a dog for company. He's already got my cat."

Dwayne laughed, and Felicity basked in the sound of it, wishing she was with him so she could kiss him and snuggle into his strong chest and smell the masculine scent of his cologne. Tears pricked her eyes. *How much longer do I need to be here, Lord?* she wondered.

"So I'm calling," she said once he'd quieted. "Because Momma's cleared to take her radiation pill next Thursday."

"That's great news."

"Yeah, it is." For a few days there, Felicity was sure her mother would break her iodine-free diet. It was really hard to only eat chicken and broccoli for every meal. No bananas. No raisins. No dairy. No bread. "Honestly, it's a miracle any of us survived the iodine diet."

Felicity had wanted to offer as much support as she could, and she'd found a few bread recipes that didn't use wheat. But her baking skills weren't as vast as she'd thought, and the bread hadn't turned out.

She and her brothers had stockpiled forbidden foods in the barn and eaten them with the doors locked.

"Anyway, she can't be around any kids for seven days. We can't use the same bathroom as her. My uncle is going to drive her home after she takes the pill, because he has a mini-van and she has to ride in the very back. We've bought every sour candy in the county."

"Sounds like you're ready."

Felicity felt tired just thinking about everything she'd done to get ready. "She should be okay to eat Christmas dinner with us. You're still comin', right?"

"I'll be there."

She exhaled, her chest loosening as if she'd expected him to say he wasn't coming anymore. She'd gone to the ranch a couple of times over the past two months, but their visits were always too short and made her too sad.

"And then I'd like to be here for another month or so just to make sure she's really doing okay."

"So we're still thinking end of January before you move back here."

"Yep."

He remained silent for several seconds, and she wondered what he could possibly be working out in his mind.

"All right," he drawled. "Well, I love you, Felicity. I'm real glad about your mom."

Felicity said, "Love you too," hung up, and pressed the phone over her heart. The end of January. She could make it to the end of January.

DWAYNE PACED FROM THE BACK DOOR OF HIS PARENTS' HOUSE TO the front. Of *his* house. "This is your house now," he muttered to himself. The homestead still didn't quite feel like home—and he knew why.

It wouldn't feel complete without Felicity here. Nothing did.

A lot had been happening in the months Felicity had been gone, and he hadn't told her about any of it. How would she react when she found out his parents had moved into her bungalow on Bartlett Street?

What would she do when she discovered that Dwayne lived in the big house now, and that he'd just hired a service to come clean out the property where he used to live on the edge of the grass so that she could live there?

Heather had assured him it was the most romantic thing he could possibly do—providing a place for her to live until they got married. Putting all the pieces in place so that all she had to do was work with horses and show up on their wedding day. But Dwayne wondered if everything he'd done to make her life as easy as possible would make her feel caged instead. Forced into the life *he* wanted her to have, not the one *she* wanted for herself.

After all, he'd promised her they'd talk about everything, make every decision together.

On his next pass through the kitchen, his eyes caught on the black ring box sitting on the single sheet of paper. He'd labored over both, spending long hours at the jewelry store here in Grape Seed Falls, and then driving to Austin to look in the bigger ring shops there. It had taken every ounce of his willpower to stay on the right highway and not head out to Marysville and ask Felicity what kind of diamond she liked.

Again, Heather had assured him that he'd done fine with the marquis cut, the thick gold band, the row of extra diamonds along the top of the ring.

Still, Dwayne couldn't help feeling a little sick to his stomach. He picked up the ring box and cracked the lid, the sight of the diamond slightly soothing. He set the ring down and picked up the list he'd been working on. With every phone call Felicity made, he learned more and more about what kind of chores she liked, and which ones she'd probably rather have him do. He'd redone the list at least half a dozen times, but he was starting to feeling like he was getting pretty close to something he could present to her.

His mind raced, his emotions spiraled, and he picked up his phone. After it went to his sister's voicemail, he said, "Tell me again why I can't propose while I'm in Marysville for Christmas."

Heather didn't call him back once school ended. Oh, no. She appeared out at the ranch, darkening the doorway of the barn where he was putting away Stockton, the horse he'd been breaking since he'd finished with Payday.

"Proposing to her at Christmas is a bad idea, because it'll forever pollute the holiday."

Dwayne frowned and unlatched the cinch. "Pollute? Getting engaged is a good thing." He was practically salivating to do it. "That makes it sound dirty."

"Have you two discussed an engagement?" She took a step into the barn and held up one finger as if checking off a list. "No. Have you told her you've already bought a ring?" Another finger went up. "No. Have you so much as mentioned that you have The Loft reserved for September?"

Dwayne flinched and lifted his eyes from the saddle. "How did you find out about The Loft?"

"Please," she said. "I work in an all-female building. When The Loft gets reserved, we all know about it."

"Too presumptuous?"

"Definitely." Heather grinned at him and crossed her arms. "Just *talk* to her already. You can discuss an engagement over the phone. Or in a text. You're not breaking up with her."

Dwayne shook his head. For some reason, he wanted the proposal to be a surprise. Probably because then Felicity couldn't freak out, back out, and break his heart.

CHRISTMAS CAME, AND DWAYNE DROVE TO MARYSVILLE, THE ring box in his glove compartment. His nerves felt like someone had put them through a tree shredder—one he'd just used a couple of days ago to get rid of some debris around the ranch.

Heather had warned him not to propose at Christmas, but Dwayne wanted to bring the ring just in case. In case of what, he wasn't sure.

He wiped his palms down his thighs as he walked toward the front door, and when Felicity opened the door and stepped onto the front porch, all his fears and doubts disappeared. "You're more beautiful than I remember." He swept her into his arms and lifted her right off her feet. "It's so good to see you."

She held onto his shoulders, tipped her head back, and laughed. "I'm so glad you made it."

"How's your mom feeling?"

"So much better," Felicity said. "She's got some sores in her mouth and nose, but that's normal." She leaned in closer. "She complains about the sour candy, but we all know she loves it." The teasing sparkle in her dark eyes sent heat right through Dwayne.

He couldn't wait another moment to kiss her, so he didn't. She melted into him, matched the tempo of his mouth, and fisted her fingers in his jacket to bring him even closer.

"Felicity," he whispered, his lips catching against hers. "I wanted to talk to you about something."

"Right now?" She pressed into him again and kissed him like she hadn't seen him in months, which of course, she hadn't.

"Yes." He put a couple of inches between them, his brain firing on all cylinders just to keep up with the conversation.

He had beautiful words rehearsed. All lined up. But all he could think of now when faced with the woman he loved was, "I want to get married as soon as possible after you return to Grape Seed Falls."

Surprise paraded across Felicity's face. She obviously hadn't been expecting marriage to be the topic, and Dwayne mentally kicked himself for bringing it up. His sister had been right, blast it.

"Married?"

"We've talked about a family," he said. "We need to get married to do that."

"Yeah, I know, sure." She stepped away from him and slicked her hair back with her palm. "How soon after I come back?"

"How long will it take you to plan a wedding?"

Pure panic poured across her face now, and Dwayne could only appreciate that she wasn't hiding it from him. She sputtered and seemed to fold into herself when she hugged her arms around her middle.

"Forget it," Dwayne said. "Let's go inside. It smells like chocolate." He moved to step past her, but she blocked him.

"I can't forget it." She gazed up at him, her fear fading. "I want to get married. I do. I just...need some time to wrap my head around it." She tipped up on her toes and grazed her mouth across his. "You understand that, don't you?"

If anyone did, it was him. He nodded, forced a smile to his lips, and said, "Of course, Felicity. Whatever you need." But something writhed inside him. Something that demanded to know what *he* needed, and how he could get it without pushing her away.

CHAPTER TWENTY-FIVE

Dwayne enjoyed Christmas with Felicity and her family. The food was good, and it turned out that he was really good at hearts, a card game she and her brothers took *very* seriously. Parker had pouted about his loss all through pie and ice cream—until Dwayne told him about King and that he should come ride the bay at the ranch.

Felicity took him shopping on Boxing Day, and they laughed and held hands and wandered the streets. Near the end of the day, she squeezed his hand and said, "There's a jewelry store right there. You wanna go in?"

Dwayne couldn't find the words to tell her that he'd already bought a ring. "Sure." He let her lead him into the store, already well-versed with the display cases, the diamond cuts, and the ring sizes.

But Felicity wasn't, and she asked a lot of questions and even tried on a few rings. Dwayne was relieved to see her asking for "more traditional gold," and that she didn't seem to prefer one cut above the other.

He did learn that she needed a size eight, and he vowed to get her ring ready for her as soon as he got home. They left the store without buying anything, and Dwayne pulled her into his side. "That was fun."

"You know what? It was." She giggled and leaned further into him. "I'll admit I was scared when you said *married* yesterday."

"Why?"

"It just hasn't been on my mind. That's all."

Dwayne approached his truck and paused. "I have more to tell you," he said. "A lot has changed around Grape Seed Ranch since you left."

Her eyebrows lifted and she said, "It has?"

"I'll start with the easy stuff." He opened the door and gestured for her to climb in.

"Start talkin'," she said as she boosted herself into the cab.

He leaned into the truck and put his hand on her knee. "My parents moved out of the homestead, and I moved into it."

FELICITY WATCHED AS DWAYNE GRINNED, CLOSED THE DOOR, and went around the front of the truck to get behind the steering wheel.

"You're pretty proud of yourself, aren't you?" She gave him a mock glare. "Moving without telling me."

He lifted one strong shoulder in a sexy half-shrug and started the truck.

"Who's livin' in your house?" she asked.

He cleared his throat and wouldn't look at her.

"Dwayne," she said, a healthy amount of warning in her voice. That familiar fear struck her right between the ribs again, and she was really starting to dislike it.

He drove a block in silence, then another.

"Dwayne." She didn't mean to whine, but there was a definitely upper pitch in her voice.

"I was hopin' you'd be moving into my house."

She opened her mouth to say something, but nothing came out.

"You know, before we get married. Then, of course, you'll be livin' in the homestead too." He spoke in a low voice she'd never heard him use before. A flush crawled up his neck and stained his cheeks.

Felicity found him adorable, and she reminded herself that he was everything she wanted, the man she loved. She slid across the bench seat and laced her arm in his.

"And for full disclosure," he said in that same, strange voice. "My parents, uh...." He coughed though he was nowhere near sick. Felicity's nerves jumped like oil in a hot pan.

"My parents are living in your house on Bartlett Street."

Whatever Felicity had been thinking he'd say, that wasn't it. "What?"

"They bought it."

"They bought it?"

"Levi helped me and my dad move your stuff over to my old house. Capri got it cleaned up before my parents moved in."

Felicity couldn't believe her best friend in Grape Seed Falls hadn't said a word about this. "How long ago?"

"Oh, a few weeks now." He glanced at her as he pulled onto the road leading out to her ranch. "The owners wanted to sell the house, and this solved a lot of problems. Are you upset?"

"No...." Upset wasn't the right word. Much like yesterday, she simply needed more time to absorb everything he'd said. Think about what it would be like to live a hundred yards from his back door. "Just processing."

He pulled under the bluebonnet arch and into the driveway. "So now probably isn't a great time to talk about this list I've been working on...."

"List?" Feliticy was tired of asking questions. "Not more horses."

He flashed a quick smile. "Oh, honey, there will always be more horses." He laughed, and she certainly wasn't upset with the prospect of more horses in her life.

"But this is about splitting up our household tasks."

Felicity gaped at him. Sure, she'd been taking care of her mother, some things in the house, and a lot on the ranch. But she honestly hadn't given much thought to what she could handle once she and Dwayne started a family. The concept of it felt very far away, and yet, here he sat, perfectly serious about this topic—and having spent a great deal of time thinking about it and preparing *a list*.

"Nope, not a good time." He got out of the truck and waited for her to join him, but she couldn't move. Dwayne chuckled and reached for her. "C'mon, sweetheart. Don't freak out."

She went with him, because he was strong when she felt weak. She wanted to be beside him, and he took her out into the ranch, her hand secured in his. He said nothing, and she enjoyed the silence as well.

Her mind wasn't quiet though. She remembered riding side-by-side with Dwayne. Throwing pennies into the wishing well. Simply walking along a fence and expecting wild horses to follow them.

They reached the wild bluebonnets and she faced him. "Dwayne, let's go get a ring."

He blinked at her, which caused her to giggle.

"I want a ring," she said. "And when I move back to Grape Seed Falls, we'll figure out our task list and how to plan a wedding. Together." The idea of putting together such a huge event by herself was completely overwhelming, but with him beside her, it didn't feel so huge, so all-encompassing.

"All right," he said, turning and taking a couple of steps. He spun back to her. "You're serious?"

She took his face in her hands and kissed him. "I'm serious."

They walked faster back to the truck than they had meandering out to the bluebonnets. He opened the passenger-side door but didn't step back to let her climb up. Instead he reached inside and opened the glove compartment.

When he faced her again, he looked like he'd swallowed dynamite and was about to explode. He dropped to one knee, and her heart hammered out of control.

"My sister is goin' to kill me," he muttered. "But you said you wanted a ring, and I sort of already have one for you." He cracked the lid on the little black box to reveal a diamond twice as big as the ones she'd just looked at.

"I love you with all my heart. Felicity Lightburne, will you marry me? Be my wife, my partner, my horse trainer, the mother of my children, my everything?"

He gazed at her with hope and happiness, fear and worry.

She had never wanted anything as much as she wanted to be his. And that thought wasn't caging or suffocating, but liberating.

"Yes," she said in a strong, sure voice. "Yes, I'll be yours."

He stood and kissed her, and Felicity had never felt quite so whole as she did while kissing her fiancé.

The End

BOOKS IN THE GRAPE SEED FALLS ROMANCE SERIES:

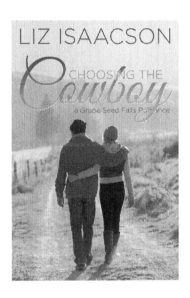

Choosing the Cowboy (Book 1): With financial trouble and personal issues around every corner, can Maggie Duffin and Chase Carver rely on their faith to find their happily-ever-after?

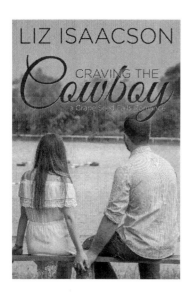

LIZ ISAACSON

CRAVING THE
Cowboy

a Grape Seed Falls Romance

Craving the Cowboy (Book 2): Dwayne Carver is set to inherit his family's ranch in the heart of Texas Hill Country, and in order to keep up with his ranch duties and fulfill his dreams of owning a horse farm, he hires top trainer Felicity Lightburne. They get along great, and she can envision herself on this new farm—at least until her mother falls ill and she has to return to help her. Can Dwayne and Felicity work through their differences to find their happily-ever-after?

BOOKS IN THE STEEPLE RIDGE ROMANCE SERIES:

Starting Over at Steeple Ridge: Steeple Ridge Romance (Book 1): Tucker Jenkins has had enough of tall buildings, traffic, and has traded in his technology firm in New York City for Steeple Ridge Horse Farm in rural Vermont. Missy Marino has worked at the farm since she was a teen, and she's always dreamed of owning it. But her ex-husband left her with a truckload of debt, making her fantasies of owning the farm unfulfilled. Tucker didn't come to the country to find a new wife, but he supposes a woman could help him start over in Steeple Ridge. Will Tucker and Missy be able to navigate the shaky ground between them to find a new beginning?

Finding Love at Steeple Ridge: A Butters Brothers Novel, Steeple Ridge Romance (Book 2): Ben Buttars is the youngest of the four Buttars brothers who come to Steeple Ridge Farm, and he finally feels like he's landed somewhere he can make a life for himself. Reagan Cantwell is a decade older than Ben and the recreational direction for the town of Island Park. Though Ben is young, he knows what he wants—and that's Rae. Can she figure out how to put what matters most in her life—family and faith—above her job before she loses Ben?

LIZ ISAACSON

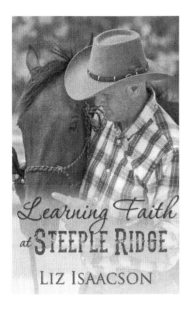

Learning Faith at Steeple Ridge: A Butters Brothers Novel, Steeple Ridge Romance (Book 3): Sam Buttars has spent the last decade making sure he and his brothers stay together. They've been at Steeple Ridge for a while now, but with the youngest married and happy, the siren's call to return to his parents' farm in Wyoming is loud in Sam's ears. He'd just go if it weren't for beautiful Bonnie Sherman, who roped his heart the first time he saw her. Do Sam and Bonnie have the faith to find comfort in each other instead of in the people who've already passed?

Learning Faith at Steeple Ridge: A Butters Brothers Novel, Steeple Ridge Romance (Book 4): Logan Buttars has always been good-natured and happy-go-lucky. After watching two of his brothers settle down, he recognizes a void in his life he didn't know about. Veterinarian Layla Guyman has appreciated Logan's friendship and easy way with animals when he comes into the clinic to get the service dogs. But with his future at Steeple Ridge in the balance, she's not sure a relationship with him is worth the risk. Can she rely on her faith and employ patience to tame Logan's wild heart?

Coming Home

to STEEPLE RIDGE

LIZ ISAACSON

Learning Faith at Steeple Ridge: A Butters Brothers Novel, Steeple Ridge Romance (Book 5): Darren Buttars is cool, collected, and quiet—and utterly devastated when his girlfriend of nine months, Farrah Irvine, breaks up with him because he wanted her to ride her horse in a parade. But Farrah doesn't ride anymore, a fact she made very clear to Darren. She returned to her childhood home with so much baggage, she doesn't know where to start with the unpacking. Darren's the only Buttars brother who isn't married, and he wants to make Island Park his permanent home—with Farrah. Can they find their way through the heartache to achieve a happily-ever-after together?

BOOKS IN THE GOLD VALLEY ROMANCE SERIES:

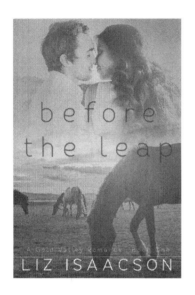

Before the Leap: A Gold Valley Romance (Book 1): Jace Lovell only has one thing left after his fiancé abandons him at the altar: his job at Horseshoe Home Ranch. Belle Edmunds is back in Gold Valley and she's desperate to build a portfolio that she can use to start her own firm in Montana. Jace isn't anywhere near forgiving his fiancé, and he's not sure he's ready for a new relationship with someone as fiery and beautiful as Belle. Can she employ her patience while he figures out how to forgive so they can find their own brand of happily-ever-after?

After the Fall: A Gold Valley Romance (Book 2): Professional snowboarder Sterling Maughan has sequestered himself in his family's cabin in the exclusive mountain community above Gold Valley, Montana after a devastating fall that ended his career. Norah Watson cleans Sterling's cabin and the more time they spend together, the more Sterling is interested in all things Norah. As his body heals, so does his faith. Will Norah be able to trust Sterling so they can have a chance at true love?

Through the Mist: A Gold Valley Romance (Book 3): Landon Edmunds has been a cowboy his whole life. An accident five years ago ended his successful rodeo career, and now he's looking to start a horse ranch--and he's looking outside of Montana. Which would be great if God hadn't brought Megan Palmer back to Gold Valley right when Landon is looking to leave. Megan and Landon work together well, and as sparks fly, she's sure God brought her back to Gold Valley so she could find her happily ever after. Through serious discussion and prayer, can Landon and Megan find their future together?

Be sure to check out the spinoff series, the Brush Creek Brides romances after you read THROUGH THE MIST. Start with A WEDDING FOR THE WIDOWER.

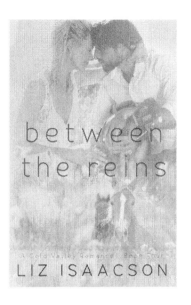

Between the Reins: A Gold Valley Romance (Book 4): Twelve years ago, Owen Carr left Gold Valley—and his long-time girlfriend—in favor of a country music career in Nashville. Married and divorced, Natalie teaches ballet at the dance studio in Gold Valley, but she never auditioned for the professional company the way she dreamed of doing. With Owen back, she realizes all the opportunities she missed out on when he left all those years ago—including a future with him. Can they mend broken bridges in order to have a second chance at love?

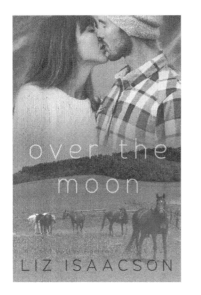

Over the Moon: A Gold Valley Romance (Book 5): Caleb Chamberlain has spent the last five years recovering from a horrible breakup, his alcoholism that stemmed from it, and the car accident that left him hospitalized. He's finally on the right track in his life—until Holly Gray, his twin brother's ex-fiance mistakes him for Nathan. Holly's back in Gold Valley to get the required veterinarian hours to apply for her graduate program. When the herd at Horseshoe Home comes down with pneumonia, Caleb and Holly are forced to work together in close quarters. Holly's over Nathan, but she hasn't forgiven him—or the woman she believes broke up their relationship. Can Caleb and Holly navigate such a rough past to find their happily-ever-after?

Journey to Steeple Ridge Farm with Holly—and fall in love with the cowboys there in the Steeple Ridge Romance series! Start with STARTING OVER AT STEEPLE RIDGE.

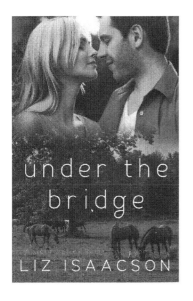

Under the Bridge: A Gold Valley Romance (Book 6): Ty Barker has been dancing through the last thirty years of his life-- and he's suddenly realized he's alone. River Lee Whitely is back in Gold Valley with her two little girls after a divorce that's left deep scars. She has a job at Silver Creek that requires her to be able to ride a horse, and she nearly tramples Ty at her first lesson. That's just fine by him, because River Lee is the girl Ty has never gotten over. Ty realizes River Lee needs time to settle into her new job, her new home, her new life as a single parent, but going slow has never been his style. But for River Lee, can Ty take the necessary steps to keep her in his life?

Up on the Housetop: A Gold Valley Romance (Book 7): Archer Bailey has already lost one job to Emersyn Enders, so he deliberately doesn't tell her about the cowhand job up at Horseshoe Home Ranch. Emery's temporary job is ending, but her obligations to her physically disabled sister aren't. As Archer and Emery work together, its clear that the sparks flying between them aren't all from their friendly competition over a job. Will Emery and Archer be able to navigate the ranch, their close quarters, and their individual circumstances to find love this holiday season?

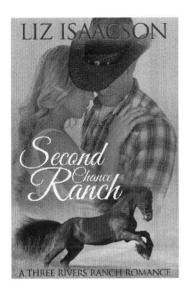

Second Chance Ranch: A Three Rivers Ranch Romance (Book 1): After his deployment, injured and discharged Major Squire Ackerman returns to Three Rivers Ranch, wanting to forgive Kelly for ignoring him a decade ago. He'd like to provide the stable life she needs, but with old wounds opening and a ranch on the brink of financial collapse, it will take patience and faith to make their second chance possible.

Third Time's the Charm: A Three Rivers Ranch Romance (Book 2): First Lieutenant Peter Marshall has a truckload of debt and no way to provide for a family, but Chelsea helps him see past all the obstacles, all the scars. With so many unknowns, can Pete and Chelsea develop the love, acceptance, and faith needed to find their happily ever after?

Fourth and Long: A Three Rivers Ranch Romance (Book 3): Commander Brett Murphy goes to Three Rivers Ranch to find some rest and relaxation with his Army buddies. Having his ex-wife show up with a seven-year-old she claims is his son is anything but the R&R he craves. Kate needs to make amends, and Brett needs to find forgiveness, but are they too late to find their happily ever after?

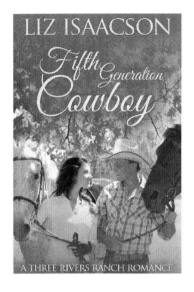

Fifth Generation Cowboy: A Three Rivers Ranch Romance (Book 4): Tom Lovell has watched his friends find their true happiness on Three Rivers Ranch, but everywhere he looks, he only sees friends. Rose Reyes has been bringing her daughter out to the ranch for equine therapy for months, but it doesn't seem to be working. Her challenges with Mari are just as frustrating as ever. Could Tom be exactly what Rose needs? Can he remove his friendship blinders and find love with someone who's been right in front of him all this time?

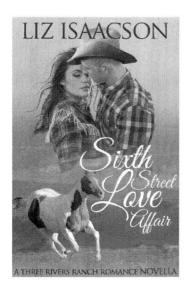

Sixth Street Love Affair: A Three Rivers Ranch Romance (Book 5): After losing his wife a few years back, Garth Ahlstrom thinks he's ready for a second chance at love. But Juliette Thompson has a secret that could destroy their budding relationship. Can they find the strength, patience, and faith to make things work?

The Seventh Sergeant: A Three Rivers Ranch Romance (Book 6): Life has finally started to settle down for Sergeant Reese Sanders after his devastating injury overseas. Discharged from the Army and now with a good job at Courage Reins, he's finally found happiness—until a horrific fall puts him right back where he was years ago: Injured and depressed. Carly Watters, Reese's new veteran care coordinator, dislikes small towns almost as much as she loathes cowboys. But she finds herself faced with both when she gets assigned to Reese's case. Do they have the humility and faith to make their relationship more than professional?

Eight Second Ride: A Three Rivers Ranch Romance (Book 7): Ethan Greene loves his work at Three Rivers Ranch, but he can't seem to find the right woman to settle down with. When sassy yet vulnerable Brynn Bowman shows up at the ranch to recruit him back to the rodeo circuit, he takes a different approach with the barrel racing champion. His patience and newfound faith pay off when a friendship--and more--starts with Brynn. But she wants out of the rodeo circuit right when Ethan wants to rejoin. Can they find the path God wants them to take and still stay together?

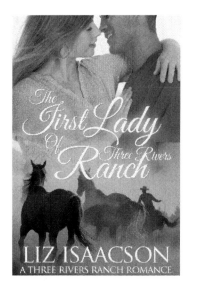

The First Lady of Three Rivers Ranch: A Three Rivers Ranch Romance (Book 8): Heidi Duffin has been dreaming about opening her own bakery since she was thirteen years old. She scrimped and saved for years to afford baking and pastry school in San Francisco. And now she only has one year left before she's a certified pastry chef. Frank Ackerman's father has recently retired, and he's taken over the largest cattle ranch in the Texas Panhandle. A horseman through and through, he's also nearing thirty-one and looking for someone to bring love and joy to a homestead that's been dominated by men for a decade. But when he convinces Heidi to come clean the cowboy cabins, she changes all that. But the siren's call of a bakery is still loud in Heidi's ears, even if she's also seeing a future with Frank. Can she rely on her faith in ways she's never had to before or will their relationship end when summer does?

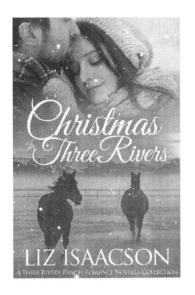

Christmas in Three Rivers: A Three Rivers Ranch Romance (Book 9): Isn't Christmas the best time to fall in love? The cowboys of Three Rivers Ranch think so. Join four of them as they journey toward their path to happily ever after in four, all-new novellas in the Amazon #1 Bestselling Three Rivers Ranch Romance series.

THE NINTH INNING: The Christmas season has never felt like such a burden to boutique owner Andrea Larsen. But with Mama gone and the holidays upon her, Andy finds herself wishing she hadn't been so quick to judge her former boyfriend, cowboy Lawrence Collins. Well, Lawrence hasn't forgotten about Andy either, and he devises a plan to get her out to the ranch so they can reconnect. Do they have the faith and humility to patch things up and start a new relationship?

TEN DAYS IN TOWN: Sandy Keller is tired of the dating scene in Three Rivers. Though she owns the pancake house, she's looking for a fresh start, which means an escape from the town where she grew up. When her older brother's best friend, Tad Jorgensen, comes to town for the holidays, it is a balm to his weary soul. A helicopter tour guide who experienced a near-death experience, he's looking to start over too--but in Three Rivers. Can Sandy and Tad navigate their troubles to find the path God wants them to take--and discover true love--in only ten days?

ELEVEN YEAR REUNION: Pastry chef extraordinaire, Grace Lewis has moved to Three Rivers to help Heidi Ackerman open a bakery in Three Rivers. Grace relishes the idea of starting over in a town where no one knows about her failed cupcakery. She doesn't expect to run into her old high school boyfriend, Jonathan Carver. A carpenter working at Three Rivers Ranch, Jon's in town against his will. But with Grace now on the scene, Jon's thinking life in Three Rivers is suddenly looking up. But with her focus on baking and his disdain for small towns, can they make their eleven year reunion stick?

THE TWELFTH TOWN: Newscaster Taryn Tucker has had enough of life on-screen. She's bounced from town to town before arriving in Three Rivers, completely alone and completely anony-mous--just the way she now likes it. She takes a job cleaning at Three Rivers Ranch, hoping for a chance to figure out who she is and where God wants her. When she meets happy-go-lucky cowhand Kenny Stockton, she doesn't expect sparks to fly. Kenny's always been "the best friend" for his female friends, but the pull between him and Taryn can't be denied. Will they have the courage and faith necessary to make their opposite worlds mesh?

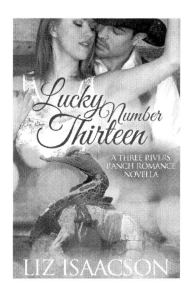

Lucky Number Thirteen: A Three Rivers Ranch Romance (Book 10): Tanner Wolf, a rodeo champion ten times over, is excited to be riding in Three Rivers for the first time since he left his philandering ways and found religion. Seeing his old friends Ethan and Brynn is therapuetic--until a terrible accident lands him in the hospital. With his rodeo career over, Tanner thinks maybe he'll stay in town--and it's not just because his nurse, Summer Hamblin, is the prettiest woman he's ever met. But Summer's the queen of first dates, and as she looks for a way to make a relationship with the transient rodeo star work Summer's not sure she has the fortitude to go on a second date. Can they find love among the tragedy?

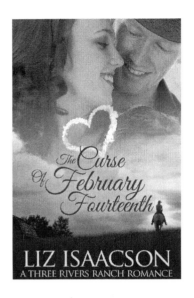

The Curse of February Fourteenth: A Three Rivers Ranch Romance (Book 11): Cal Hodgkins, cowboy veterinarian at Bowman's Breeds, isn't planning to meet anyone at the masked dance in small-town Three Rivers. He just wants to get his bachelor friends off his back and sit on the sidelines to drink his punch. But when he sees a woman dressed in gorgeous butterfly wings and cowgirl boots with blue stitching, he's smitten. Too bad she runs away from the dance before he can get her name, leaving only her boot behind...

BOOKS IN THE BRUSH CREEK BRIDES ROMANCE SERIES:

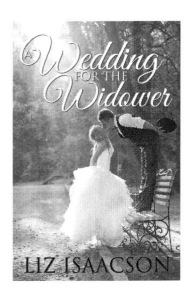

A Wedding for the Widower: Brush Creek Brides Romance (Book 1): Former rodeo champion and cowboy Walker Thompson trains horses at Brush Creek Horse Ranch, where he lives a simple life in his cabin with his ten-year-old son. A widower of six years, he's worked with Tess Wagner, a widow who came to Brush Creek to escape the turmoil of her life to give her seven-year-old son a slower pace of life. But Tess's breast cancer is back...

Walker will have to decide if he'd rather spend even a short time with Tess than not have her in his life at all. Tess wants to feel God's love and power, but can she discover and accept God's will in order to find her happy ending?

A Companion for the Cowboy: Brush Creek Brides Romance (Book 2): Cowboy and professional roper Justin Jackman has found solitude at Brush Creek Horse Ranch, preferring his time with the animals he trains over dating. With two failed engagements in his past, he's not really interested in getting his heart stomped on again. But when flirty and fun Renee Martin picks him up at a church ice cream bar--on a bet, no less--he finds himself more  than just a little interested. His Gen-X attitudes are attractive to her; her Millennial behaviors drive him nuts. Can Justin look past their differences and take a chance on another engagement?

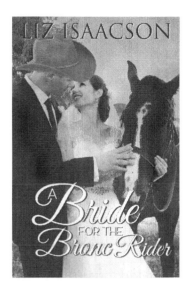

A Bride for the Bronc Rider: Brush Creek Brides Romance (Book 3): Ted Caldwell has been a retired bronc rider for years, and he thought he was perfectly happy training horses to buck at Brush Creek Ranch. He was wrong. When he meets April Nox, who comes to the ranch to hide her pregnancy from all her friends back in Jackson Hole, Ted realizes he has a huge family-shaped hole in his life. April is embarrassed, heartbroken, and trying to find her extinguished faith. She's never ridden a horse and wants nothing to do with a cowboy ever again. Can Ted and April create a family of happiness and love from a tragedy?

A Family for the Farmer: Brush Creek Brides Romance (Book 4): Blake Gibbons oversees all the agriculture at Brush Creek Horse Ranch, sometimes moonlighting as a general contractor. When he meets Erin Shields, new in town, at her aunt's bakery, he's instantly smitten. Erin moved to Brush Creek after a divorce that left her penniless, homeless, and a single mother of three children under age eight. She's nowhere near ready to start dating again, but the longer Blake hangs around the bakery, the more she starts to like him. Can Blake and Erin find a way to blend their lifestyles and become a family?

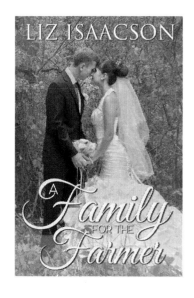

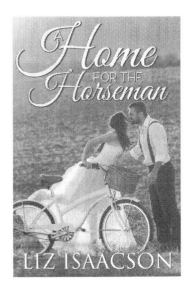

A Home for the Horseman: Brush Creek Brides Romance (Book 5): Emmett Graves has always had a positive outlook on life. He adores training horses to become barrel racing champions during the day and cuddling with his cat at night. Fresh off her professional rodeo retirement, Molly Brady comes to Brush Creek Horse Ranch as Emmett's protege. He's not thrilled, and she's allergic to cats. Oh, and she'd like to stay cowboy-free, thank you very much. But Emmett's about as cowboy as they come.... Can Emmett and Molly work together without falling in love?

A Refuge for the Rancher: Brush Creek Brides Romance (Book 6): Grant Ford spends his days training cattle—when he's not camped out at the elementary school hoping to catch a glimpse of his ex-girlfriend. When principal Shannon Sharpe confronts him and asks him to stay away from the school, the spark between them is instant and hot. Shannon's expecting a transfer very soon, but she also needs a summer outdoor coordinator—

and Grant fits the bill. Just because he's handsome and everything Shannon's ever wanted in a cowboy husband means nothing. Will Grant and Shannon be able to survive the summer or will the Utah heat be too much for them to handle?

ABOUT LIZ

Liz Isaacson writes inspirational romance, usually set in Texas, or Montana, or anywhere else horses and cowboys exist. She lives in Utah, where she teaches elementary school, taxis her daughter to dance several times a week, and eats a lot of Ferrero Rocher while writing. Find her on her website at lizisaacson.com.